# CRITICAL ACCLAIM FOR THE MOST IMPORTANT AND SHATTERING PLAY OF THE YEAR!

LARRY KRAMER wrote the screenplay adaptation and produced the film version of ...... e, which received four Aca..... ing Best Screenplay, and w...... . He is the author of the nove...... eal of controversy upon ...... become one of the best-selling of ...... lm executive for Columbia and United Artists, he has worked on numerous film scripts and productions, most of them in London, where he made his home for ten years. He currently lives in New York City.

941

931

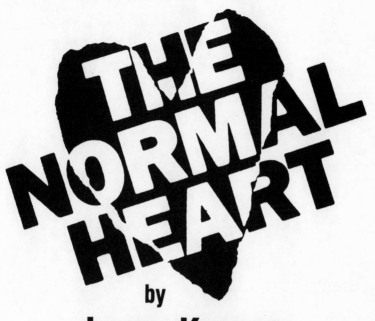

# THE NORMAL HEART

by

## Larry Kramer

With an Introduction by Andrew Holleran
and a Foreword by Joseph Papp

A PLUME BOOK

## NEW AMERICAN LIBRARY

NEW YORK AND SCARBOROUGH, ONTARIO

ACKNOWLEDGMENT
Portion of "September 1, 1939," copyright © 1940 by W. H. Auden. Reprinted from *The English Auden*, edited by Edward Mendelson, by permission of Random House, Inc.

Cover photograph by Martha Swope

Published simultaneously in Canada by
The New American Library of Canada Limited

 PLUME TRADEMARK REG. U.S. PAT. OFF. AND FOREIGN COUNTRIES
REG. TRADEMARK—MARCA REGISTRADA
HECHO EN HARRISONBURG, VA., U.S.A.

SIGNET, SIGNET CLASSIC, MENTOR, ONYX, PLUME, MERIDIAN and NAL BOOKS are published *in the United States* by NAL PENGUIN INC., 1633 Broadway, New York, New York 10019, *in Canada* by The New American Library of Canada Limited, 81 Mack Avenue, Scarborough, Ontario M1L 1M8

LIBRARY OF CONGRESS CATALOGING-IN-PUBLICATION DATA

Kramer, Larry.
    The normal heart.

    1. Acquired immune deficiency syndrome—Drama.
I. Title.
PS3561.R252N6   1985   812'.54   85-15430
ISBN 0-453-00506-3
ISBN 0-452-25798-0 (pbk.)

First Printing, October, 1985

        5   6   7   8   9   10   11   12   13

PRINTED IN THE UNITED STATES OF AMERICA

For Norman J. Levy,
who succeeded where all others failed.

The windiest militant trash
Important Persons shout
Is not so crude as our wish:
What mad Nijinsky wrote
About Diaghilev
Is true of the normal heart;
For the error bred in the bone
Of each woman and each man
Craves what it cannot have,
Not universal love
But to be loved alone.

All I have is a voice
To undo the folded lie,
The romantic lie in the brain
Of the sensual man-in-the-street
And the lie of Authority
Whose buildings grope the sky:
There is no such thing as the State
And no one exists alone;
Hunger allows no choice
To the citizen or the police;
We must love one another or die.

*From* "September 1, 1939"
W. H. AUDEN

Original New York Production of
*The Normal Heart*
by New York Shakespeare Festival.

Produced by Joseph Papp.

# ACKNOWLEDGMENTS

Theater is an especially collaborative endeavor. Many people help to make a play.

I would like to thank: Arthur Kramer (as always), A. J. Antoon, Ann and Don Brown, Michael Callen, Michael Carlisle, Joseph Chaikin, Kate Costello, Dr. James D'Eramo, Helen Eisenbach, Dr. Roger Enlow, Tom Erhardt, Robert Ferro, Emmett Foster, Jim Fouratt, Sanford Friedman, Dr. Alvin Friedman-Kien, Dr. Patrick Hennessey, Richard Howard, Jane Isay, Dr. Richard Isay, Chuck Jones, Owen Laster, Dr. Frank Lilly, Joan and David Maxwell, Rodger McFarlane, Patrick Merla, Hermine and Maurice Nessen, Mike Nichols, Nick Olcott, Charles Ortleb, Johnnie Planco, Judy Prince, Margaret Ramsay, Mary Anne and Douglas Schwalbe, Will Schwalbe, Dr. Joseph Sonnabend, and Tim Westmoreland.

I particularly thank my intelligent cast, and our director, Michael Lindsay-Hogg, a humble, gentle man of great patience and courage.

I give special thanks and tribute to Dr. Linda J. Laubenstein.

I am grateful to the following works of scholarship: "American Jewry During the Holocaust," a report edited by Seymour Maxwell Finger for the American Jewish Commission on the Holocaust, Hon. Arthur J. Goldberg, Chairman, March 1984, (the excerpt quoted herein is used by permission); *Israel in the Mind of America* by Peter Grose, Alfred A. Knopf, 1983; *American Jewry's Public Response to the Holocaust, 1938–44*: An Examination Based upon Accounts in the Jewish Press and Periodical Literature, A Doctoral Dissertation by Haskel

Lookstein, Yeshiva University, January 1979, University Microfilms, Ann Arbor, Michigan; *While Six Million Died, A Chronicle of American Apathy*, by Arthur D. Morse, copyright © 1967, The Overlook Press, Woodstock, New York, 1983; *The Abandonment of the Jews, America and the Holocaust, 1941-1945*, by David S. Wyman, Pantheon Books, 1984.

For encouraging, challenging, inspiring, and teaching me— for caring—I am exceptionally indebted to Gail Merrifield, the Director of Plays at the New York Shakespeare Festival, as I am to this remarkable organization's Literary Manager, Bill Hart.

Indeed, there is not a person at the New York Shakespeare Festival to whom I cannot say, Thank you.

There are no words splendid enough to contain and convey what Joseph Papp has meant to me, and to this play.

There are many people who lived this play, who lived these years, and who live no more. I miss them.

—LARRY KRAMER

*The Normal Heart* opened on April 21, 1985 at the Public Theater in New York City, New York; a New York Shakespeare Festival Production, it was produced by Joseph Papp. It had the following cast:

## Cast of Characters
### *(IN ORDER OF APPEARANCE)*

| | |
|---|---|
| CRAIG DONNER | *Michael Santoro* |
| MICKEY MARCUS | *Robert Dorfman* |
| NED WEEKS | *Brad Davis\** |
| DAVID | *Lawrence Lott* |
| DR. EMMA BROOKNER | *Concetta Tomei* |
| BRUCE NILES | *David Allen Brooks* |
| FELIX TURNER | *D. W. Moffett* |
| BEN WEEKS | *Phillip Richard Allen* |
| TOMMY BOATWRIGHT | *William DeAcutis* |
| HIRAM KEEBLER | *Lawrence Lott* |
| GRADY | *Michael Santoro* |
| EXAMINING DOCTOR | *Lawrence Lott* |
| ORDERLY | *Lawrence Lott* |
| ORDERLY | *Michael Santoro* |
| | |
| Director | *Michael Lindsay-Hogg* |
| Scenery | *Eugene Lee and Keith Raywood* |
| Lighting | *Natasha Katz* |
| Costumes | *Bill Walker* |
| Associate Producer | *Jason Steven Cohen* |

*The action of this play takes place between July 1981 and May 1984 in New York City.*

* On August 19, 1985, Joel Grey assumed the role of Ned Weeks.

# Scenes and Approximate Dates

## ACT ONE

## ACT TWO

# About the Production

The New York Shakespeare Festival production at the Public Theater was conceived as exceptionally simple. Little furniture was used: a few wooden office chairs, a desk, a table, a sofa, and an old battered hospital gurney that found service as an examining table, a bench in City Hall, and a place for coats in the organization's old office. As the furniture found itself doing double-duty in different scenes, so did the doorways built into the set's back wall. In many instances, the actors used the theater itself for entrances and exits.

The walls of the set, made of construction-site plywood, were whitewashed. Everywhere possible, on this set and upon the theater walls too, facts and figures and names were painted, in black, simple lettering.

Here are some of the things we painted on our walls:

1. Principal place was given to the latest total number of AIDS cases nationally: _____ AND COUNT-ING. (For example, on August 1, 1985, the figure read 12,062.)

    As the Centers for Disease Control revise all figures regularly, so did we, crossing out old numbers and placing the new figure just beneath it.

2. This was also done for states and major cities.

3. EPIDEMIC OFFICIALLY DECLARED JUNE 5, 1981.

4. MAYOR KOCH: $75,000—MAYOR FEINSTEIN: $16,000,000. (For public education and community services.)

5. "TWO MILLION AMERICANS ARE IN- FECTED—ALMOST 10 TIMES THE OFFICIAL ESTIMATES"—Dr. Robert Gallo, London *Observer*, April 7, 1985.

6. The number of cases in children.

7. The number of cases in gays and the number of cases in straights, calculated by subtracting the gay and bi- sexual number from the total CDC figure.

8. The total number of articles on the epidemic written by the following newspapers during the first ten months of 1984:
   *The San Francisco Chronicle* .......................... 163
   *The New York Times* ..................................... 41
   *The Los Angeles Times* ................................. 37
   *The Washington Post* .................................... 24

9. During the first nineteen months of the epidemic, *The New York Times* wrote about it a total of seven times:
   1. July 3, 1981, page 20 (41 cases reported by CDC)
   2. August 29, 1981, page 9 (107 cases)
   3. May 11, 1982, Section III, page 1 (335 cases)
   4. June 18, 1982, Section II, page 8 (approximately 430 cases)
   5. August 8, 1982, page 31 (505 cases)
   6. January 6, 1983, Section II, page 17 (approxi- mately 891 cases)

7.  February 6, 1983, Magazine (The "Craig Clai-
    borne" article.) (958 cases)

10. During the three months of the Tylenol scare in 1982,
    *The New York Times* wrote about it a total of 54 times:
    October 1, 2, 3, 4, 5, 6, 7, 8, 9, 10, 11, 12, 13, 14, 15,
       16, 17, 18, 19, 20, 21, 22, 23, 24, 25, 26, 27, 28, 29,
       30, 31
    November 2, 5, 6, 9, 12, 17, 21, 22, 25
    December 1, 2, 3, 4, 8, 10, 14, 15, 19, 25, 27, 28, 29,
       30
    Four of these articles appeared on the front page.
    Total number of cases: 7.

11. Government research at the National Institutes of
    Health did not commence in reality until January, 1983,
    eighteen months after the same government had de-
    clared the epidemic.

12. One entire wall contained this passage:
    "There were two alternative strategies a Jewish
    organization could adopt to get the American gov-
    ernment to initiate action on behalf of the imperiled
    Jews of Europe. It could cooperate with the govern-
    ment officials, quietly trying to convince them that
    rescue of Jews should be one of the objectives of the
    war, or it could try to pressure the government into
    initiating rescue by using embarrassing public atten-
    tion and rallying public opinion to that end.
       The American Jewish Committee chose the for-
    mer strategy and clung to it tenaciously.
       From the very onset of Jewish crises, the Com-
    mittee responded to each new Nazi outrage by prac-
    ticing their traditional style of discreet 'backstairs'
    diplomacy.

With each worsening event, the Committee re-acted by contacting yet another official or re-visiting the same ones to call their attention to the new situation.

The Jewish delegates were usually politely informed that the matter was being given the 'most earnest attention.'

They were still trying to persuade the same officials when the war ended."

> From "American Jewry During the Holocaust"
> Prepared for the American Jewish Commission
> on the Holocaust, 1984, Edited by
> Seymour Maxwell Finger

13. Announcement of the discovery of "the virus" in France: January, 1983.

    Announcement of the "discovery" of "the virus" in Washington: April, 1984.

14. The public education budget for 1985 at the U.S. Department of Health and Human Services: $120,000.

15. Vast expanses of wall were covered with lists of names, much like the names one might find on a war memorial, such as the Vietnam Memorial in Washington.

The most current case totals can be obtained by telephoning the Centers for Disease Control in Atlanta, 404-329-3162.

*The New York Native* also publishes up-to-date figures in each issue.

# Introduction

Shortly after Larry Kramer co-founded the Gay Men's Health Crisis, he came out to Fire Island one sunny Saturday and set up a stand by the harbor to collect donations. It was one of those sparkling Saturdays when life was so cheerful that Larry's appeal seemed more like a petition to save the dunes than a warning which made any deep impression. The friend I was with who stopped to chat with Larry died three years later, but the whole subject that moment—the water lapping against the dock, the men in Speedos walking by with groceries, Larry squinting into the sunlight—seemed esoteric and unthreatening; so esoteric that when Larry appeared in the *New York Native* soon after this with an article on the epidemic ("1,112 And Counting"), a reader promptly wrote in to accuse him of peddling the gospel that the wages of sin are death. Larry Kramer had a reputation, you know—for writing *Faggots*, a novel some felt in 1978 was negative (and others found accurate)—so that when he reappeared a few years later warning homosexuals that having sex with one another was now possibly lethal, no one took it kindly. *That's Larry*, was the word around town: *always screaming*.

He was plainly upset when I visited him one day in his apartment on Washington Square; he also said he felt guilty allowing these meetings, fund-raisers, feuds, to keep him from his typewriter. At the time the Gay Men's Health Crisis sounded vaguely like a church social (Were any of the members cute? we asked), and the whole brouhaha tangential to the life I and my friends lived—no one we knew was sick. Indeed, not only was AIDS still so rare that homosexuals in other cities considered it a New York problem—like high rents, or the IRT—it took *chutzpah* to go out to the Pines and appear among the sailboats, striped awnings, and men in Speedos with a suggestion that the party was over. Gay life was booming at the time: more gyms, more discos, more faces and bodies than ever before. The first person I know of to get sick was one of its exemplars: the owner of his own clothing store on Columbus Avenue, a set-builder who had a close family of friends, a boyfriend, a talent for giving parties and enjoying life. He got, among other things, herpes of the brain, and died. Then his boyfriend shriveled up: a bright architect with a superb physique. Then a famous model, and then a warm, funny, talented neighbor down the street, and then the friend who'd stopped by Larry's stand to chat before we went to the grocery store.

This taught me something important about AIDS: the only way it ceases to be a news story is this—you, or someone you care for, gets it. Then it is transformed, immediately, from a bizarre, depressing media topic into a fact that is indescribably cruel. The next time I visited Larry my interest in what he knew about this disease was no longer academic: I wanted to know what he thought of such-and-such a treatment, this hospital, that doctor. But he'd had some sort of fight with GMHC and been kicked out of the group he'd helped found. For a while he returned to the novel he'd been working on before all this: tried it as a screenplay, then turned it back into a novel—but, like the tossing and turning of the literary form, he himself seemed unable to return to business as usual. Because nothing was usual anymore—and the community at

large did not want to hear. Articles about AIDS seemed shrill—
hosts of dinner parties refused to allow the topic in conversation. But what other topic was there? The writer who sat
down to treat one of the themes which till now had formed
our conversation and literature—the manners, the morals of
gay life—felt as if he were discussing the fine points of a
bridge game in the lounge while the *Titanic* was going down.
No words could banish the Kaposi's sarcoma my friend showed
me one afternoon on the street by suddenly pulling up his lip:
dark and purple as grapes, hanging down from the gum above
his teeth.

No amount of denial could, either—yet the fact that sex
and cancer were twins was so unnerving that most people
wanted to ignore it. Americans on some level believe the
gravest danger facing them is our failure to floss before bed-
time. At the beginning of this century Henry James was struck
by the number of people eating candy bars when he visited
New York; seventy years later, we were not eating candy bars
(they were fattening), we were munching on people. There
was no limit to the amount of sex one could have in New
York—that was one of the things that made the city so ex-
citing. And yet when the plague began—and there were people who insisted it not be called a plague—I thought it must
change things irrevocably. The owner of the most popular
bathhouse in Manhattan knew his community better when he
predicted: "People will go on doing the same things, but with
more anxiety." After all, the basis of the whole culture was
sex. (As it is of any culture.) The smart turned celibate. Others
became more orgiastic. But most were Jekyll & Hyde; rational,
health-conscious, aware, we went from the news of some death
in all its horrifying detail directly to the baths, and then home
to lie awake till dawn wondering if this was the Killer Trick.
Life in Manhattan by 1982 began to resemble the tale of Edgar

Allan Poe: Death had arrived at the ball, and it wore a mask. And when we weren't wondering which mask it was, we were asking, silently, if this disease was merely a medical fact which had no moral implications or—to put it bluntly—our fault. For *Faggots* had not exactly inspired a debate; gay life had gone on to surpass its dark comedy, and no one even now wanted to face the fact that they might have to abstain from sex or to demand that our taxes be used to cure this new affliction.

Millions of our fellow citizens, of course, were sure this illness was nothing more, or less, than what homosexuals deserved: a kind of divine leprosy. To be avoided by the television crews who refused to interview people with AIDS, the firemen who asked for masks, the undertakers who would not accept the bodies. The human capacity to care about the deaths of anyone but ourselves, or those close to us, is not very great—and society at large seemed at best uninterested. An illness whose targets were Haitians, homosexuals, drug addicts, and hemophiliacs was not the sort telethons are built around. It was their problem. (When Secretary Heckler declared at an AIDS conference that we must stop the disease before it spread to the heterosexual population, she was only inadvertently articulating the general view that homosexuals live and die apart from the rest of us.) The media that responded instantly to the illness of a group of Legionnaires holding a convention at a hotel in Philadelphia inserted this story somewhat farther from the front page: as if this epidemic was merely a penalty for sex and belonged—like Hester Prynne gathering mushrooms—in the forest outside of town.

At the same time—to complete the horrid vaudeville—there were homosexuals saying this was a plot by the CIA to deny them a fundamental right: promiscuity. As the deaths went on, and on, both sides seemed equally mad. And all the theories we formed to keep it away from us (that only extremely drugged sex junkies of a certain generation got it) were eliminated. Blacks thought whites had given it to them. Whites thought vice-versa. Young men were telling their families in the same breath: "I am homosexual, and have cancer." People were stoically enduring attempted cures so harsh that not only did the therapy (we know now) hasten their deaths, but they were a treatment, one man said just before dying, "worse than the disease." Try to imagine, if you can, the individual horror. The hospitals. The blood. The feeling that this was life's final prize for having been homosexual. The wondering how your friends would behave, how you would tell your family, what all this had been for. While a small fraction of the community cared for those too weak to argue with insurance companies, ride a bus to the doctor, go to the grocery store or shave, most of us simply went on in shock wondering when the time bomb in our blood would go off, while others, to whom Manhattan was now a cemetery, abandoned the city to escape an existence in which sex and death were synonomous.

When Larry left New York after his dismissal from the group he helped found, he acquired a car, a dog, began to drive around the country, and finally resolved the feud between his life and writing. *The Normal Heart* is, after all, a history play—of the past five years: a period in which thousands died. There is really nothing more to say to introduce a play in which you will find virtually every fact, statistic, issue, anguish, lament, and question alluded to here. Neither is there any way to regard or discuss this play as drama. (Though one cannot help notice it asks the same questions *Faggots* raised eight years ago.) It is a hunk of reality which has been depicted for us, so current that, to paraphrase a film critic, the sirens you hear on stage are the sirens you hear when you walk out of the theater. It is a play which relies, to an extraordinary degree, on what actually happened and what actually was said. What actually happened and what actually was said were awful—which is why *The Normal Heart* is painful to see, and upsetting to read. But then, as the author said to me recently, "This is not a play about measles." It is about something the Africans call the Horror.

—ANDREW HOLLERAN

# Foreword

Larry Kramer's *The Normal Heart* is a play in the great tradition of Western drama. In taking a burning social issue and holding it up to public and private scrutiny so that it reverberates with the social and personal implications of that issue, *The Normal Heart* reveals its origins in the theater of Sophocles, Euripides, and Shakespeare. In his moralistic fervor, Larry Kramer is a first cousin to nineteenth-century Ibsen and twentieth-century Odets and other radical writers of the 1930s. Yet, at the heart of *The Normal Heart*, the element that gives this powerful political play its essence, is love—love holding firm under fire, put to the ultimate test, facing and overcoming our greatest fear: death.

I love the ardor of this play, its howling, its terror and its kindness. It makes me very proud to be its producer and caretaker.

—JOSEPH PAPP

# ACT ONE

## Scene 1

*The office of* DR. EMMA BROOKNER. *Three men are in the waiting area:* CRAIG DONNER, MICKEY MARCUS, *and* NED WEEKS.

CRAIG: *(After a long moment of silence.)* I know something's wrong.

MICKEY: There's nothing wrong. When you're finished we'll go buy you something nice. What would you like?

CRAIG: We'll go somewhere nice to eat, okay? Did you see that guy in there's spots?

MICKEY: You don't have those. Do you?

CRAIG: No.

MICKEY: Then you don't have anything to worry about.

CRAIG: She said they can be inside you, too.

MICKEY: They're not inside you.

CRAIG: They're inside me.

MICKEY: Will you stop! Why are you convinced you're sick?

CRAIG: Where's Bruce? He's supposed to be here. I'm so lucky to have such a wonderful lover. I love Bruce so much, Mickey. I know something's wrong.

MICKEY:  Craig, all you've come for is some test results. Now stop being such a hypochondriac.

CRAIG:  I'm tired all the time. I wake up in swimming pools of sweat. Last time she felt me and said I was swollen. I'm all swollen, like something ready to explode. Thank you for coming with me, you're a good friend. Excuse me for being such a mess, Ned. I get freaked out when I don't feel well.

MICKEY:  Everybody does.

(DAVID *comes out of* EMMA'*s office. There are highly visible purple lesions on his face. He wears a long-sleeved shirt. He goes to get his jacket, which he's left on one of the chairs.*)

DAVID:  Whoever's next can go in.

CRAIG:  Wish me luck.

MICKEY:  (*Hugging* CRAIG.) Good luck.

(CRAIG *hugs him, then* NED, *and goes into* EMMA'*s office.*)

DAVID:  They keep getting bigger and bigger and they don't go away. (*To* NED.) I sold you a ceramic pig once at Maison France on Bleecker Street. My name is David.

NED:  Yes, I remember. Somebody I was friends with then collects pigs and you had the biggest pig I'd ever seen outside of a real pig.

DAVID:  I'm her twenty-eighth case and sixteen of them are dead. (*He leaves.*)

NED:  Mickey, what the fuck is going on?

MICKEY:  I don't know. Are you here to write about this?

NED:  I don't know. What's wrong with that?

MICKEY:  Nothing, I guess.

NED: What about you? What are you going to say? You're the one with the health column.

MICKEY: Well, I'll certainly write about it in the *Native*, but I'm afraid to put it in the stuff I write at work.

NED: What are you afraid of?

MICKEY: The city doesn't exactly show a burning interest in gay health. But at least I've still got my job: the Health Department has had a lot of cutbacks.

NED: How's John?

MICKEY: John? John who?

NED: You've had so many I never remember their last names.

MICKEY: Oh, you mean John. I'm with Gregory now. Gregory O'Connor.

NED: The old gay activist?

MICKEY: Old? He's younger than you are. I've been with Gregory for ten months now.

NED: Mickey, that's very nice.

MICKEY: He's not even Jewish. But don't tell my rabbi.

CRAIG: (*Coming out of* EMMA's *office.*) I'm going to die. That's the bottom line of what she's telling me. I'm so scared. I have to go home and get my things and come right back and check in. Mickey, please come with me. I hate hospitals. I'm going to die. Where's Bruce? I want Bruce.

(MICKEY *and* CRAIG *leave.* DR. EMMA BROOKNER *comes in from her office. She is in a motorized wheelchair. She is in her mid-to-late thirties.*)

EMMA: Who are you?

NED: I'm Ned Weeks. I spoke with you on the phone after the *Times* article.

EMMA:   You're the writer fellow who's scared. I'm scared, too. I hear you've got a big mouth.

NED:   Is big mouth a symptom?

EMMA:   No, a cure. Come on in and take your clothes off.

(*Lights up on an examining table, center stage.* NED *starts to undress.*)

NED:   Dr. Brookner, what's happening?

EMMA:   I don't know.

NED:   In just a couple of minutes you told two people I know something. The article said there isn't any cure.

EMMA:   Not even any good clues yet. And even if they found out tomorrow what's happening, it takes years to find out how to cure and prevent anything. All I know is this disease is the most insidious killer I've ever seen or studied or heard about. And I think we're seeing only the tip of the iceberg. And I'm afraid it's on the rampage. I'm frightened nobody important is going to give a damn because it seems to be happening mostly to gay men. Who cares if a faggot dies? Does it occur to you to do anything about it. Personally?

NED:   Me?

EMMA:   Somebody's got to do something.

NED:   Wouldn't it be better coming from you?

EMMA:   Doctors are extremely conservative; they try to stay out of anything that smells political, and this smells. Bad. As soon as you start screaming you get treated like a nut case. Maybe you know that. And then you're ostracized and rendered worthless, just when you need cooperation most. Take off your socks.

(NED, *in his undershorts, is now sitting on the examining table.* EMMA *will now examine him, his skin particularly, starting with the bottom of his feet, feeling his lymph glands, looking at his scalp, into his mouth . . .)*

NED: Nobody listens for very long anyway. There's a new disease of the month every day.

EMMA: This hospital sent its report of our first cases to the medical journals over a year ago. *The New England Journal of Medicine* has finally published it, and last week, which brought you running, the *Times* ran something on some inside page. Very inside: page twenty. If you remember, Legionnaires' Disease, toxic-shock, they both hit the front page of the *Times* the minute they happened. And stayed there until somebody did something. The front page of the *Times* has a way of inspiring action. Lie down.

NED: They won't even use the word "gay" unless it's in a direct quote. To them we're still homosexuals. That's like still calling blacks Negroes. The *Times* has always had trouble writing about anything gay.

EMMA: Then how is anyone going to know what's happening? And what precautions to take? Someone's going to have to tell the gay population fast.

NED: You've been living with this for over a year? Where's the Mayor? Where's the Health Department?

EMMA: They know about it. You have a Commissioner of Health who got burned with the Swine Flu epidemic, declaring an emergency when there wasn't one. The government appropriated $150 million for that mistake. You have a Mayor who's a bachelor and I assume afraid of being perceived as too friendly to anyone gay. And who is also out to protect a billion-dollar-a-year tourist industry. He's not about to tell the world there's an epidemic menacing his city. And don't ask me about the President. Is the Mayor gay?

NED:  If he is, like J. Edgar Hoover, who would want him?

EMMA:  Have you had any of the symptoms?

NED:  I've had most of the sexually transmitted diseases the article said come first. A lot of us have. You don't know what it's been like since the sexual revolution hit this country. It's been crazy, gay or straight.

EMMA:  What makes you think I don't know? Any fever, weight loss, night sweats, diarrhea, swollen glands, white patches in your mouth, loss of energy, shortness of breath, chronic cough?

NED:  No. But those could happen with a lot of things, couldn't they?

EMMA:  And purple lesions. Sometimes. Which is what I'm looking for. It's a cancer. There seems to be a strange reaction in the immune system. It's collapsed. Won't work. Won't fight. Which is what it's supposed to do. So most of the diseases my guys are coming down with—and there are some very strange ones—are caused by germs that wouldn't hurt a baby, not a baby in New York City anyway. Unfortunately, the immune system is the system we know least about. So where is this big mouth I hear you've got?

NED:  I have more of a bad temper than a big mouth.

EMMA:  Nothing wrong with that. Plenty to get angry about. Health is a political issue. Everyone's entitled to good medical care. If you're not getting it, you've got to fight for it. Do you know this is the only country in the industrialized world besides South Africa that doesn't guarantee health care for everyone? Open your mouth. Turn over. One of my staff told me you were well-known in the gay world and not afraid to say what you think. Is that true? I can't find any gay leaders. I tried calling several gay organizations. No one ever calls me back. Is anyone out there?

NED: There aren't any organizations strong enough to be useful, no. Dr. Brookner, nobody with a brain gets involved in gay politics. It's filled with the great unwashed radicals of any counterculture. That's why there aren't any leaders the majority will follow. Anyway, you're talking to the wrong person. What I think is politically incorrect.

EMMA: Why?

NED: Gay is good to that crowd, no matter what. There's no room for criticism, looking at ourselves critically.

EMMA: What's your main criticism?

NED: I hate how we play victim, when many of us, most of us, don't have to.

EMMA: Then you're exactly what's needed now.

NED: Nobody ever listens. We're not exactly a bunch that knows how to play follow the leader.

EMMA: Maybe they're just waiting for somebody to lead them.

NED: We are. What group isn't?

EMMA: You can get dressed. I can't find what I'm looking for.

NED: (*Jumping down and starting to dress.*) Needed? Needed for what? What is it exactly you're trying to get me to do?

EMMA: Tell gay men to stop having sex.

NED: What?

EMMA: Someone has to. Why not you?

NED: It is a preposterous request.

EMMA: It only sounds harsh. Wait a few more years, it won't sound so harsh.

NED: Do you realize that you are talking about millions of men who have singled out promiscuity to be their principal political agenda, the one they'd die before abandoning. How do you deal with that?

EMMA:   Tell them they may die.

NED:   You tell them!

EMMA:   Are you saying you guys can't relate to each other in a nonsexual way?

NED:   It's more complicated than that. For a lot of guys it's not easy to meet each other in any other way. It's a way of connecting—which becomes an addiction. And then they're caught in the web of peer pressure to perform and perform. Are you sure this is spread by having sex?

EMMA:   Long before we isolated the hepatitis viruses we knew about the diseases they caused and had a good idea of how they got around. I think I'm right about this. I am seeing more cases each week than the week before. I figure that by the end of the year the number will be doubling every six months. That's something over a thousands cases by next June. Half of them will be dead. Your two friends I've just diagnosed? One of them will be dead. Maybe both of them.

NED:   And you want me to tell every gay man in New York to stop having sex?

EMMA:   Who said anything about just New York?

NED:   You want me to tell every gay man across the country—

EMMA:   Across the world! That's the only way this disease will stop spreading.

NED:   Dr. Brookner, isn't that just a tiny bit unrealistic?

EMMA:   Mr. Weeks, if having sex can kill you, doesn't anybody with half a brain stop fucking? But perhaps you've never lost anything. Good-bye.

(BRUCE NILES, *an exceptionally handsome man in his late thirties, rushes in carrying* CRAIG, *helped by* MICKEY.)

BRUCE:  (*Calling from off.*) Where do I go? Where do I go?

EMMA:  Quickly—put him on the table. What happened?

BRUCE:  He was coming out of the building and he started running to me and then he ... then he collapsed to the ground.

EMMA:  What is going on inside your bodies!

(CRAIG *starts to convulse.* BRUCE, MICKEY, *and* NED *restrain him.*)

EMMA:  Gently. Hold on to his chin.

(*She takes a tongue depressor and holds* CRAIG's *tongue flat; she checks the pulse in his neck; she looks into his eyes for vital signs that he is coming around;* CRAIG's *convulsions stop.*)

You the lover?

BRUCE:  Yes.

EMMA:  What's your name?

BRUCE:  Bruce Niles, ma'am.

EMMA:  How's your health?

BRUCE:  Fine. Why—is it contagious?

EMMA:  I think so.

MICKEY:  Then why haven't you come down with it?

EMMA:  (*Moving toward a telephone.*) Because it seems to have a very long incubation period and require close intimacy. Niles? You were Reinhard Holz's lover?

BRUCE:  How did you know that? I haven't seen him in a couple of years.

EMMA:  (*Dialing the hospital emergency number.*) He died three weeks ago. Brookner. Emergency. Set up a room immediately.

(*Hangs up.*)

BRUCE:    We were only boyfriends for a couple months.

MICKEY:    It's like some sort of plague.

EMMA:    There's always a plague. Of one kind or another. I've had it since I was a kid. Mr. Weeks, I don't think your friend is going to live for very long.

---

# Scene 2

FELIX TURNER's *desk at* The New York Times. FELIX *is always conservatively dressed, and is outgoing and completely masculine.*

NED:    (*Entering, a bit uncomfortable and nervous.*) Mr. Turner?

FELIX:    Bad timing. (*Looking up.*) "Mister?"

NED:    My name is Ned Weeks.

FELIX:    You caught me at a rough moment. I have a deadline.

NED:    I've been told you're gay and might be able to help get vital information in the *Times* about—

FELIX:    You've been told? Who told you?

NED:    The grapevine.

FELIX:    Here I thought everyone saw me as the Burt Reynolds of West Forty-third Street. Please don't stop by and say hello to Mr. Sulzberger or Abe Rosenthal. What kind of vital information?

NED:   You read the article about this new disease?

FELIX:   Yes, I read it. I wondered how long before I'd hear from somebody. Why does everyone gay always think I run *The New York Times*? I can't help you ... with this.

NED:   I'm sorry to hear that. What would you suggest I do?

FELIX:   Take your pick. I've got twenty-three parties, fourteen gallery openings, thirty-seven new restaurants, twelve new discos, one hundred and five spring collections ... Anything sound interesting?

NED:   No one here wants to write another article. I've talked to half a dozen reporters and editors and the guy who wrote the first piece.

FELIX:   That's true. They won't want to write about it. And I can't. We're very departmentalized. You wouldn't want science to write about sweaters, would you?

NED:   It is a very peculiar feeling having to go out and seek support from the straight world for something gay.

FELIX:   I wouldn't know about that. I just write about gay designers and gay discos and gay chefs and gay rock stars and gay photographers and gay models and gay celebrities and gay everything. I just don't call them gay. Isn't that enough for doing my bit?

NED:   No—I don't think it's going to be.

FELIX:   I really do have a deadline and you wouldn't like me to get fired; who would write about us at all?

NED:   Guys like you give me a pain in the ass. (*He starts out.*)

FELIX:   Are you in the book?

NED:   Yes.

---

# Scene 3

*The law office of* BEN WEEKS, NED's *older brother.* BEN *always dresses in a suit and tie, which* NED *never does. The brothers love each other a great deal;* BEN's *approval is essential to* NED. BEN *is busy with some papers as* NED, *sitting on the opposite side of the desk, waits for him.*

BEN:   Isn't it a bit early to get so worked up?

NED:   Don't you be like that, too?

BEN:   What have I done now?

NED:   My friend Bruce and I went out to Fire Island and over the whole Labor Day weekend we collected the grand sum of $124.

BEN:   You can read that as either an indication that it's a beginning and will improve, or as a portent that heads will stay in the sand. My advice is heads are going to stay in the sand.

NED:   Because so many gay people are still in the closet?

BEN:   Because people don't like to be frightened. When they get scared they don't behave well. It's called denial. (*Giving* NED *some papers to sign.*)

NED:   (*Signs them automatically.*) What are these for?

BEN: Your account needs some more money. You never seem to do anything twice. One movie, one novel, one play... You know you are now living on your capital. I miss your being in the movie business. I like movies. (*Unrolls some blueprints.*)

NED: What are those?

BEN: I've decided to build a house.

NED: But the one you're in is terrific.

BEN: I just want to build me a dream house, so now I'm going to.

NED: It looks like a fortress. Does it have a moat? How much is it going to cost?

BEN: I suspect it'll wind up over a million bucks. But you're not to tell that to anyone. Not even Sarah. I've found some land in Greenwich, by a little river, completely protected by trees. Ned, it's going to be beautiful.

NED: Doesn't spending a million dollars on a house frighten you? It would scare the shit out of me. Even if I had it.

BEN: You can have a house anytime you want one. You haven't done badly.

NED: Do I detect a tinge of approval—from the big brother who always called me lemon?

BEN: Well, you were a lemon.

NED: I don't want a house.

BEN: Then why have you been searching for one in the country for so many years?

NED: It's no fun living in one alone.

BEN: There's certainly no law requiring you to do that. Is this... Bruce someone you're seeing?

NED:   Why thank you for asking. Don't I wish. I see him. He just doesn't see me. Everyone's afraid of me anyway. I frighten them away. It's called the lemon complex.

BEN:   I think you're the one who's scared.

NED:   You've never said that before.

BEN:   Yes, I have. You just didn't hear me. What's the worst thing that could happen to you.

NED:   I'd spend a million bucks on a house. Look, Ben— please! (*He takes the blueprints from him.*) I've—we've started an organization to raise money and spread information and fight any way we can.

BEN:   Fight who and what?

NED:   I told you. There's this strange new disease...

BEN:   You're not going to do that full-time?

NED:   I just want to help it get started and I'll worry about how much time later on.

BEN:   It sounds to me like another excuse to keep from writing.

NED:   I knew you would say that. I was wondering... could your law firm incorporate us and get us tax-exempt status and take us on for free, what's it called, *pro bono*?

BEN:   *Pro bono* for what? What are you going to do?

NED:   I just told you—raise money and fight.

BEN:   You have to be more specific than that. You have to have a plan.

NED:   How about if we say we're going to become a cross between the League of Women Voters and the United States Marines? Is that a good-enough plan?

BEN: Well, we have a committee that decides this sort of thing. I'll have to put it to the committee.

NED: Why can't you just say yes?

BEN: Because we have a committee.

NED: But you're the senior partner and I'm your brother.

BEN: I fail to see what bearing that has on the matter. You're asking me to ask my partners to give up income that would ordinarily come into their pocket.

NED: I thought every law firm did a certain amount of this sort of thing—charity, worthy causes.

BEN: It's not up to me, however, to select just what these worthy causes might be.

NED: Well, that's a pity. What did you start the firm for?

BEN: That's one of our rules. It's a democratic firm.

NED: I think I like elitism better. When will you know?

BEN: Know what?

NED: Whether or not your committee wants to help dying faggots?

BEN: I'll put it to them at the next meeting.

NED: When is that?

BEN: When it is!

NED: When is it? Because if you're not going to help, I have to find somebody else.

BEN: You're more than free to do that.

NED: I don't want to do that! I want my big brother's fancy famous big-deal straight law firm to be the first major New York law firm to do *pro bono* work for a gay cause. That would give me a great deal of pride. I'm sorry you can't see that.

I'm sorry I'm still putting you in a position where you're ashamed of me. I thought we'd worked all that out years ago.

BEN: I am not ashamed of you! I told you I'm simply not free to take this on without asking my partners' approval at the next meeting.

NED: Why don't I believe that. When is the next meeting?

BEN: Next Monday. Can you wait until next Monday?

NED: Who else is on the committee?

BEN: What difference does that make?

NED: I'll lobby them. You don't seem like a very sure vote. Is Nelson on the committee? Norman Ivey? Harvey?

BEN: Norman and Harvey are.

NED: Good.

BEN: Okay? Lemon, where do you want to have lunch today? It's your turn to pay.

NED: It is not. I paid last week.

BEN: That's simply not true.

NED: Last week was ... French. You're right. Do you know you're the only person in the world I can't get mad at and stay mad at. I think my world would come to an end without you. And then who would Ben talk to? (*He embraces* BEN.)

BEN: (*Embracing back, a bit.*) That's true.

NED: You're getting better at it.

# Scene 4

NED's *apartment. It is stark, modern, all black and white.* FELIX *comes walking in from another room with a beer, and* NED *follows, carrying one, too.*

FELIX: That's quite a library in there. You read all those books?

NED: Why does everybody ask that?

FELIX: You have a whole room of 'em, you must want to get asked.

NED: I never thought of it that way. Maybe I do. Thank you. But no, of course I haven't. They go out of print and then you can't find them, so I buy them right away.

FELIX: I think you're going to have to face the fact you won't be able to read them all before you die.

NED: I think you're right.

FELIX: You know, I really used to like high tech, but I'm tired of it now. I think I want chintz back again. Don't be insulted.

NED: I'm not. I want chintz back again, too.

FELIX: So here we are—two fellows who want chintz back again. Excuse me for saying so, but you are stiff as starch.

NED: It's been a long time since I've had a date. This is a date, isn't it? (FELIX *nods.*) And on the rare occasion, I was usually the asker.

FELIX:   That's what's thrown you off your style: I called and asked.

NED:   Some style. Before any second date I usually receive a phone call that starts with "Now I don't know what you had in mind, but can't we just be friends?"

FELIX:   No. Are you glad I'm here?

NED:   Oh, I'm pleased as punch you're here. You're very good-looking. What are you doing here?

FELIX:   I'll let that tiny bit of self-pity pass for the moment.

NED:   It's not self-pity, it's nervousness.

FELIX:   It's definitely self-pity. Do you think you're bad-looking?

NED:   Where are you from?

FELIX:   I'm from Oklahoma. I left home at eighteen and put myself through college. My folks are dead. My dad worked at the refinery in West Tulsa and my mom was a waitress at a luncheonette in Walgreen's.

NED:   Isn't it amazing how a kid can come out of all that and wind up on the *Times* dictating taste and style and fashion to the entire world?

FELIX:   And we were talking so nicely.

NED:   Talking is not my problem. Shutting up is my problem. And keeping my hands off you.

FELIX:   You don't have to keep your hands off me. You have very nice hands. Do you have any awkward sexual tendencies you want to tell me about, too? That I'm not already familiar with?

NED:   What are you familiar with?

FELIX:   I have found myself pursuing men who hurt me. Before minor therapy. You're not one of those?

NED: No, I'm the runner. I *was* the runner. Until major therapy. After people who didn't want me and away from people who do.

FELIX: Isn't it amazing how a kid can come out of all that analyzing everything incessantly down to the most infinitesimal neurosis and still be all alone?

NED: I'm sorry you don't like my Dr. Freud. Another aging Jew who couldn't get laid.

FELIX: Just relax. You'll get laid.

NED: I try being laid-back, assertive, funny, butch... What's the point? I don't think there are many gay relationships that work out anyway.

FELIX: It's difficult to imagine you being laid-back. I know a lot of gay relationships that are working out very well.

NED: I guess I never see them.

FELIX: That's because you're a basket case.

NED: Fuck off.

FELIX: What's the matter? Don't you think you're attractive? Don't you like your body?

NED: I don't think anybody really likes their body. I read that somewhere.

FELIX: You know my fantasy has always been to go away and live by the ocean and write twenty-four novels, living with someone just like you with all these books who of course will be right there beside me writing your own twenty-four novels.

NED: (*After a beat.*) Me, too.

FELIX: Harold Robbins marries James Michener.

NED: How about Tolstoy and Charles Dickens?

FELIX:   As long as Kafka doesn't marry Dostoevsky.

NED:   Dostoevsky is my favorite writer.

FELIX:   I'll have to try him again.

NED:   If you really feel that way, why do you write all that society and party and fancy-ball-gown bullshit?

FELIX:   Here we go again. I'll bet you gobble it up every day.

NED:   I do. I also know six people who've died. When I came to you a few weeks ago, it was only one.

FELIX:   I'm sorry. Is that why you agreed to this date?

NED:   Do you know that when Hitler's Final Solution to eliminate the Polish Jews was first mentioned in the *Times* it was on page twenty-eight. And on page six of the *Washington Post*. And the *Times* and the *Post* were owned by Jews. What causes silence like that? Why didn't the American Jews help the German Jews get out? Their very own people! Scholars are finally writing honestly about this—I've been doing some research—and it's damning to everyone who was here then: Jewish leadership for being totally ineffective; Jewish organizations for constantly fighting among themselves, unable to cooperate even in the face of death: Zionists versus non-Zionists, Rabbi Wise against Rabbi Silver...

FELIX:   Is this some sort of special way you talk when you don't want to talk? We were doing so nicely.

NED:   We were?

FELIX:   Wasn't there an awful lot of anti-Semitism in those days? Weren't Jews afraid of rubbing people's noses in too much shit?

NED:   Yes, everybody has a million excuses for not getting involved. But aren't there moral obligations, moral com-

mandments to try everything possible? Where were the
Christian churches, the Pope, Churchill? And don't get me
started on Roosevelt . . . How I was brought up to worship
him, all Jews were. A clear statement from him would have
put everything on the front pages, would have put Hitler
on notice. But his administration did its best to stifle pub-
licity at the same time as they clamped down immigration
laws forbidding entry, and this famous haven for the oppressed became as inaccessible as Tibet. The title of Trea-
sury Secretary Morgenthau's report to Roosevelt was
"Acquiescence of This Government in the Murder of the
Jews," which he wrote in 1944. Dachau was opened in 1933.
Where was everybody for eleven years? And then it was
too late.

FELIX:    This is turning out to be a very romantic evening.

NED:    And don't tell me how much you can accomplish working from the inside. Jewish leaders, relying on their contacts
with people in high places, were still, quietly, from the
inside, attempting to persuade them when the war was over.

FELIX:    What do you want me to say? Do you ever take a
vacation?

NED:    A vacation. I forgot. That's the great goal, isn't it. A
constant Fire Island vacation. Party, party; fuck, fuck. Maybe
you can give me a few trendy pointers on what to wear.

FELIX:    Boy, you really have a bug up your ass. Look, I'm
not going to tell them I'm gay and could I write about the
few cases of a mysterious disease that seems to be standing
in the way of your kissing me even though there must be
half a million gay men in this city who are fine and healthy.
Let us please acknowledge the law of averages. And this is
not World War Two. The numbers are no where remotely

comparable. And all analogies to the Holocaust are tired, overworked, boring, probably insulting, possibly true, and a major turnoff.

NED:   Are they?

FELIX:   Boy, I think I've found myself a real live weird one. I had no idea. (*Pause.*) Hey, I just called you weird.

NED:   You are not the first.

FELIX:   You've never had a lover, have you?

NED:   Where did you get that from?

FELIX:   Have you? Wow.

NED:   I suppose you've had quite a few.

FELIX:   I had a very good one for a number of years, thank you. He was older than I was and he found someone younger.

NED:   So you like them older. You looking for a father?

FELIX:   No, I am not looking for a father! God, you are relentless. And as cheery as Typhoid Mary.

(NED *comes over to Felix and sits beside him. Then he leans over and kisses him. The kiss becomes quite intense. Then* NED *breaks away, jumps up, and begins to walk around nervously.*)

NED:   The American Jews knew exactly what was happening, but everything was downplayed and stifled. Can you imagine how effective it would have been if every Jew in America had marched on Washington? Proudly! Who says I want a lover? Huh!? I mean, why doesn't anybody believe me when I say I do not want a lover?

FELIX:   You are fucking crazy. Jews, Dachau, Final Solution—what kind of date is this! I don't believe anyone in the whole wide world doesn't want to be loved. Ned, you don't remember me, do you? We've been in bed together.

We made love. We talked. We kissed. We cuddled. We made love again. I keep waiting for you to remember, something, anything. But you don't!

NED: How could I not remember you?

FELIX: I don't know.

NED: Maybe if I saw you naked.

FELIX: It's okay as long as we treat each other like whores. It was at the baths a few years ago. You were busy cruising some blond number and I stood outside your door waiting for you to come back and when you did you gave me such an inspection up and down you would have thought I was applying for the CIA.

NED: And then what?

FELIX: I just told you. We made love twice. I thought it was lovely. You told me your name was Ned, that when you were a child you read a Philip Barry play called *Holiday* where there was a Ned, and you immediately switched from ... Alexander? I teased you for taking such a Wasp, up-in-Connecticut-for-the-weekend-name, and I asked what you did, and you answered something like you'd tried a number of things, and I asked you if that had included love, which is when you said you had to get up early in the morning. That's when I left. But I tossed you my favorite go-fuck-yourself yourself when you told me "I really am not in the market for a lover"—men do not just naturally not love—they learn not to. I am not a whore. I just sometimes make mistakes and look for love in the wrong places. And I think you're a bluffer. Your novel was all about a man desperate for love and a relationship, in a world filled with nothing but casual sex.

NED:  Do you think we could start over?

FELIX:  Maybe.

## Scene 5

NED's *apartment*. MICKEY, BRUCE, *and* TOMMY BOATWRIGHT, *a Southerner in his late twenties, are stuffing envelopes with various inserts and then packing them into cartons. Beer and pretzels.*

MICKEY:  (*Calling off.*) Ned, Gregory says hello and he can't believe you've turned into an activist. He says where were you fifteen years ago when we needed you.

NED:  (*Coming in with a tray with more beer.*) You tell Gregory fifteen years ago no self-respecting faggot would have anything to do with you guys.

TOMMY:  I was twelve years old.

BRUCE:  We're not activists.

MICKEY:  If you're not an activist, Bruce, then what are you?

BRUCE:  Nothing. I'm only in this until it goes away.

MICKEY:  You know, the battle against the police at Stonewall was won by transvestites. We all fought like hell. It's you Brooks Brothers guys who—

BRUCE:  That's why I wasn't at Stonewall. I don't have anything in common with those guys, girls, whatever you call them. Ned, Robert Stokes has it. He called me today.

NED:   At Glenn Fitzsimmons' party the other night, I saw one friend there I knew was sick, I learned about two others, and then walking home I bumped into Richie Faro, who told me he'd just been diagnosed.

MICKEY:   Richie Faro?

NED:   All this on Sixth Avenue between Nineteenth and Eighth Streets.

MICKEY:   Richie Faro—gee, I haven't seen him since Stonewall. I think we even had a little affairlet.

BRUCE:   Are you a transvestite?

MICKEY:   No, but I'll fight for your right to be one.

BRUCE:   I don't want to be one!

MICKEY:   I'm worried this organization might only attract white bread and middle-class. We need blacks...

TOMMY:   Right on!

MICKEY:   ...and...how do you feel about Lesbians?

BRUCE:   Not very much. I mean, they're...something else.

MICKEY:   I wonder what they're going to think about all this? If past history is any guide, there's never been much support by either half of us for the other. Tommy, are you a Lesbian?

TOMMY:   (*As he exits into the kitchen.*) I have done and seen everything.

NED:   (*To* BRUCE) How are you doing?

BRUCE:   I'm okay now. I forgot to thank you for sending flowers.

NED:   That's okay.

BRUCE:   Funny—my mother sent flowers. We've never even

talked about my being gay. I told her Craig died. I guess she knew.

NED:    I think mothers somehow always know. Would you like to have dinner next week, maybe see a movie?

BRUCE:    (*Uncomfortable when* NED *makes advances.*) Actually . . . it's funny . . . it happened so fast. You know Albert? I've been seeing him.

NED:    That guy in the Calvin Klein ads? Great!

(TOMMY *returns dragging another carton of envelopes and boxes.*)

BRUCE:    I don't think I like to be alone. I've always been with somebody.

MICKEY:    (*Looking up from his list-checking.*) We have to choose a president tonight, don't forget. I'm not interested. And what about a board of directors?

BRUCE:    (*Looking at one of the flyers.*) Mickey, how did you finally decide to say it? I didn't even look.

MICKEY:    I just said the best medical knowledge, which admittedly isn't very much, seems to feel that a virus has landed in our community. It could have been any community, but it landed in ours. I guess we just got in the way. Boy, are we going to have paranoia problems.

NED:    (*Looking at a flyer.*) That's all you said?

MICKEY:    See what I mean? No, I also put in the benefit dance announcement and a coupon for donations.

NED:    What about the recommendations?

MICKEY:    I recommend everyone should donate a million dollars. How are we going to make people realize this is not just a gay problem? If it happens to us, it can happen to anybody. I sent copies to all the gay newspapers.

BRUCE:    What good will that do? Nobody reads them.

MICKEY:   The *Native*'s doing a good job.

NED:   (*Who has read the flyer and is angry.*) Mickey, I thought we talked this out on the phone. We must tell everybody what Emma wants us to tell them.

MICKEY:   She wants to tell them so badly she won't lend her name as recommending it. (*To the others.*) This is what Ned wrote for me to send out. "If this doesn't scare the shit out of you, and rouse you to action, gay men may have no future here on earth." Neddie, I think that's a bit much.

BRUCE:   You'll scare everybody to death!

NED:   Shake up. What's wrong with that? This isn't something that can be force-fed gently; it won't work. Mickey neglected to read my first sentence.

MICKEY:   "It's difficult to write this without sounding alarmist or scared." Okay, but then listen to this: "I am sick of guys moaning that giving up careless sex until this blows over is worse than death . . . I am sick of guys who can only think with their cocks . . . I am sick of closeted gays. It's 1982 now, guys, when are you going to come out? By 1984 you could be dead."

BRUCE:   You're crazy.

NED:   Am I? There are almost five hundred cases now. Okay, if we're not sending it out, I'll get the *Native* to run it.

BRUCE:   But we can't tell people how to live their lives! We can't do that. And besides, the entire gay political platform is fucking. We'd get it from all sides.

NED:   You make it sound like that's all that being gay means.

BRUCE:   That's all it does mean!

MICKEY:   It's the only thing that makes us different.

NED:   I don't want to be considered different.

BRUCE:    Neither do I, actually.

MICKEY:    Well, I do.

BRUCE:    Well, you are!

NED:    Why is it we can only talk about our sexuality, and so relentlessly? You know, Mickey, all we've created is generations of guys who can't deal with each other as anything but erections. We can't even get a meeting with the mayor's gay assistant!

TOMMY:    I'm very interested in setting up some sort of services for the patients. We've got to start thinking about them.

BRUCE:    (*Whispering to* NED.) Who's he?

TOMMY:    He heard about you and he found you and here he is. My name is Tommy Boatwright... (*To* NED.) Why don't you write that down? Tommy Boatwright. In real life, I'm a hospital administrator. And I'm a Southern bitch.

NED:    Welcome to gay politics.

BRUCE:    Ned, I won't have anything to do with any organization that tells people how to live their lives.

NED:    It's not telling them. It's a recommendation.

MICKEY:    With a shotgun to their heads.

BRUCE:    It's interfering with their civil rights.

MICKEY:    Fucking as a civil right? Don't we just wish.

TOMMY:    What if we put it in the form of a recommendation from gay doctors? So that way we're just the conduit.

NED:    I can't get any gay doctor to go on record and say publicly what Emma wants.

BRUCE:    The fortunes they've made off our being sick, you'd think they could have warned us. (*Suddenly noticing an envelope.*) What the fuck is this?

MICKEY: Unh, oh!

BRUCE: Look at this! Was this your idea?

NED: I'm looking. I'm not seeing.

NED: What don't I see?

MICKEY: What we put for our return address.

NED: You mean the word gay is on the envelope?

BRUCE: You're damn right. Instead of just the initials. Who did it?

NED: Well, maybe it was Pierre who designed it. Maybe it was a mistake at the printers. But it is the name we chose for this organization...

BRUCE: You chose. I didn't want "gay" in it.

MICKEY: No, we all voted. That was one of those meetings when somebody actually showed up.

NED: Bruce, I think it's interesting that nobody noticed until now. You've been stuffing them all week at your apartment.

BRUCE: We can't send them out.

NED: We have to if we want anybody to come to the dance. They were late from the printers as it is.

BRUCE: We can go through and scratch out the word with a Magic Marker.

NED: Ten thousand times? Look, I feel sympathy for young guys still living at home on Long Island with their parents, but most men getting these...Look at you, in your case what difference does it make? You live alone, you own your own apartment, your mother lives in another state...

BRUCE:   What about my mailman?

(MICKEY *lets out a little laughing yelp, then clears his throat.*)

NED:   You don't expect me to take that seriously?

BRUCE:   Yes, I do!

NED:   What about your doorman?

BRUCE:   What about him?

NED:   Why don't you worry about him? All those cute little Calvin Klein numbers you parade under his nose, he thinks you're playing poker with the boys?

BRUCE:   You don't have any respect for anyone who doesn't think like you do, do you?

NED:   Bruce, I don't agree with you about this. I think it's imperative that we all grow up now and come out of the closet.

MICKEY:   Ladies, behave! Ned, you don't think much of our sexual revolution. You say it all the time.

NED:   No, I say I don't think much of promiscuity. And what's that got to do with gay envelopes?

MICKEY:   But you've certainly done your share.

NED:   That doesn't mean I approve of it or like myself for doing it.

MICKEY:   But not all of us feel that way. And we don't like to hear the word "promiscuous" used pejoratively.

BRUCE:   Or so publicly.

NED:   Where the world can hear it, Bruce?

MICKEY:   Sex is liberating. It's always guys like you who've never had one who are always screaming about relationships, and monogamy and fidelity and holy matrimony. What are you, a closet straight?

NED:   Mickey, more sex isn't more liberating. And having so much sex makes finding love impossible.   *Sum his views up.*

MICKEY:   Neddie, dahling, do not put your failure to find somebody on the morality of all the rest of us.

NED:   Mickey, dahling, I'm just saying what I think! It's taken me twenty years of assorted forms of therapy in various major world capitals to be able to do so without guilt, fear, or giving a fuck if anybody likes it or not.

TOMMY:   I'll buy that!

NED:   Thank you.

BRUCE:   But not everyone's so free to say what they think!

MICKEY:   Or able to afford so much therapy. Although God knows I need it. (*Looking at his watch.*) Look, it's late, and we haven't elected our president. Ned, I think it should be . . . Bruce. Everybody knows him and likes him and . . . I mean, everybody expects you to—

NED:   You mean he's popular and everybody's afraid of me.

MICKEY:   Yes.

TOMMY:   No.

MICKEY:   No.

TOMMY:   No, what it means is that you have a certain kind of energy that's definitely needed, but Bruce has a . . . presence that might bring people together in a way you can't.

NED:   What's that mean?

TOMMY:   It means he's gorgeous—and all the kids on Christopher Street and Fire Island will feel a bit more comfortable following him.

NED:   Just like high school.

TOMMY *and* MICKEY:   Yes!

NED:   Follow him where?

TOMMY:   (*Putting his arm around him.*) Well, honey, why don't we have a little dinner and I'll tell you all about it—and more.

NED:   Uhn, thanks, I'm busy.

TOMMY:   Forever? Well, that's too bad. I wanted to try my hand at smoothing out your rough edges.

MICKEY:   Good luck.

NED:   (*To Bruce.*) Well, it looks like you're the president.

BRUCE:   I don't think I want this.

NED:   Oh, come on, you're gorgeous—and we're all going to follow you.

BRUCE:   Fuck you. I accept.

NED:   Well, fuck you, congratulations.

TOMMY:   There are going to be a lot of scared people out there needing someplace to call for information. I'd be interested in starting some sort of telephone hotline.

BRUCE:   (*His first decision in office.*) Unh . . . sure. Just prepare a detailed budget and let me see it before you make any commitments.

MICKEY:   (*To* NED.) Don't you feel in safe hands already?

TOMMY:   (*To* BRUCE.) What is it you do for a living, if I may ask?

BRUCE:   I'm a vice-president of Citibank.

TOMMY:   That's nothing to be shy about, sugar. You invented the Cash Machine. (*Picking up an envelope.*) So, are we mailing these out or what?

BRUCE:   What do you think?

TOMMY:   I'll bet nobody even notices.

BRUCE:   Oh, there will be some who notice. Okay.

TOMMY:   Okay? Okay! Our first adult compromise. Thank
y'all for your cooperation.

(FELIX, *carrying a shopping bag, lets himself in with his own key.*
NED *goes to greet him.*)

NED:   Everybody, this is Felix. Bruce, Tommy, Mickey. Bruce
just got elected president.

FELIX:   My condolences. Don't let me interrupt. Anybody
wants any Balducci gourmet ice cream—it's eighteen bucks
a pint?

(NED *and* FELIX *go into the kitchen.*)

MICKEY:   It looks like Neddie's found a boyfriend.

BRUCE:   Thank God, now maybe he'll leave me alone.

TOMMY:   Shit, he's got his own key. It looks like I signed on
too late.

BRUCE:   I worry about Ned. I mean, I like him a lot, but his
style is so . . . confrontational. We could get into a lot of
trouble with him.

TOMMY:   Honey, he looks like a pretty good catch to me. We
could get into a lot of trouble without him.

(NED *and* FELIX *come back.* FELIX *cleans up after the guys.*)

MICKEY:   I'm going home. My Gregory, he burns dinner every
night, and when I'm late, he blames me.

BRUCE:   (*To* NED.) My boss doesn't know and he hates gays.
He keeps telling me fag jokes and I keep laughing at them.

NED:   Citibank won't fire you for being gay. And if they did,
we could make such a stink that every gay customer in New

York would leave them. Come on, Bruce—you used to be a fucking Green Beret!

TOMMY:   Goodness!

BRUCE:   But I love my job. I supervise a couple thousand people all over the country and my investments are up to twenty million now.

MICKEY:   I'm leaving. (*He hefts a carton and starts out.*)

BRUCE:   Wait, I'm coming. (*To* NED.) I just think we have to stay out of anything political.

(FELIX *goes back into the kitchen.*)

NED:   And I think it's going to be impossible to pass along *any* information or recommendation that isn't going to be considered political by somebody.

TOMMY:   And I think this is not an argument you two boys are going to settle tonight.

(BRUCE *starts out and as he passes* NED, NED *stops him and kisses him good-bye on the mouth.* BRUCE *picks up a big carton and heads out.*)

TOMMY:   (*Who has waited impatiently for Bruce to leave so he can be alone with Ned.*) I just wanted to tell you I really admire your writing . . . and your passion . . . (*As* FELIX *reenters from the kitchen,* TOMMY *drops his flirtatious tone.*) . . . and what you've been saying and doing, and it's because of you I'm here. (*To* FELIX.) Take care this good man doesn't burn out. Good night. (*He leaves.*)

NED:   We just elected a president who's in the closet. I lost every argument. And I'm the only screamer among them. Oh, I forgot to tell them—I'm getting us something on the local news.

FELIX:   Which channel?

NED:   It's not TV, it's radio...It's a start.

FELIX:   Ned, I think you should have been president.

NED:   I didn't really want it. I've never been any good playing on a team. I like stirring things up on my own. Bruce will be a good president. I'll shape him up. Where's the ice cream? Do you think I'm crazy?

FELIX:   I certainly do. That's why I'm here.

NED:   I'm so glad.

FELIX:   That I'm here?

NED:   That you think I'm crazy. (*They kiss.*)

# Scene 6

BEN's *office. In a corner is a large model of the new house under a cloth cover.*

BEN:   You got your free legal work from my firm; now I'm not going to be on your board of directors, too.

NED:   I got our free legal work from your firm by going to Norman and he said, "Of course, no problem." I asked him, "Don't you have to put it before your committee?" And he said, "Nah, I'll just tell them we're going to do it."

BEN: Well...you got it.

NED: All I'm asking for is the use of your name. You don't have to do a thing. This is an honorary board. For the stationery.

BEN: Ned, come on—it's your cause, not mine.

NED: That is just an evasion!

BEN: It is not. I don't ask you to help me with the Larchmont school board, do I?

NED: But I would if you asked me.

BEN: But I don't.

NED: Would you be more interested if you thought this was a straight disease?

BEN: It has nothing to do with your being gay.

NED: Of course it has. What else has it got to do with?

BEN: I've got other things to do.

NED: But I'm telling you you don't have to do a thing!

BEN: The answer is No.

NED: It's impossible to get this epidemic taken seriously. I wrote a letter to the gay newspaper and some guy wrote in, "Oh there goes Ned Weeks again; he wants us all to die so he can say 'I told you so.'"

BEN: He sounds like a crazy.

NED: It kept me up all night.

BEN: Then you're crazy, too.

NED: I ran into an old friend I hadn't seen in years in the subway, and I said, "Hello, how are you?" He started screaming, "You're giving away all our secrets, you're painting us as sick, you're destroying homosexuality"—and then he tried to slug me. Right there in the subway. Under Bloomingdale's.

BEN: Another crazy.

NED: We did raise $50,000 at our dance last week. That's more money than any gay organization has ever raised at one time in this city before.

BEN: That's wonderful, Ned. So you must be beginning to do something right.

NED: And I made a speech appealing for volunteers and we got over a hundred people to sign up, including a few women. And I've got us on Donahue. I'm going to be on Donahue with a doctor and a patient.

BEN: Don't tell your mother.

NED: Why not?

BEN: She's afraid someone is going to shoot you.

(BEN *rolls the model house stage center and pulls off the cover.*)

NED: What about you? Aren't you afraid your corporate clients will say, "Was that your faggot brother I saw on TV?" Excuse me—is this a bad time? You seem preoccupied.

BEN: Do I? I'm sorry. A morning with the architect is enough to shake me up a little bit. It's going to cost more than I thought.

NED: More?

BEN: Twice as much.

NED: Two million?

BEN: I can handle it.

NED: You can? That's very nice. You know, Ben, one of these

days I'll make you agree that over twenty million men and women are not all here on this earth because of something requiring the services of a psychiatrist.

BEN:  Oh, it's up to twenty million now, is it? Every time we have this discussion, you up the ante.

NED:  We haven't had this discussion in years, Ben. And we grow, just like everybody else.

BEN:  Look, I try to understand. I read stuff. (*Picking up a copy of* Newsweek, *with "Gay America" on the cover.*) I open magazines and I see pictures of you guys in leather and chains and whips and black masks, with captions saying this is a social worker, this is a computer analyst, this is a schoolteacher—and I say to myself, "This isn't Ned."

NED:  No, it isn't. It isn't most of us. You know the media always dramatizes the most extreme. Do you think we all wear dresses, too?

BEN:  Don't you?

NED:  Me, personally? No, I do not.

BEN:  But then you tell me how you go to the bathhouses and fuck blindly, and to me that's not so different from this. You guys don't seem to understand why there are rules, and regulations, guidelines, responsibilities. You guys have a dreadful image problem.

NED:  I know that! That's what has to be changed. That's why it's so important to have people like you supporting us. You're a respected person. You already have your dignity.

BEN:  We better decide where we're going to eat lunch and get out of here. I have an important meeting.

NED:  Do you? How important? I've asked for your support.

BEN: In every area I consider important you have my support.

NED: In some place deep inside of you you still think I'm sick. Isn't that right? Okay. Define it for me. What do you mean by "sick"? Sick unhealthy? Sick perverted? Sick I'll get over it? Sick to be locked up?

BEN: I think you've adjusted to life quite well.

NED: All things considered? (BEN *nods*.) In the only area I consider important I don't have your support at all. The single-minded determination of all you people to forever see us as sick helps keep us sick.

BEN: I saw how unhappy you were!

NED: So were you! You wound up going to shrinks, too. We grew up side by side. We both felt pretty much the same about Mom and Pop. I refuse to accept for one more second that I was damaged by our childhood while you were not.

BEN: But we all don't react the same way to the same thing.

NED: That's right. So I became a writer and you became a lawyer. I'll agree to the fact that I have any number of awful character traits. But not to the fact that whatever they did to us as kids automatically made me sick and gay while you stayed straight and healthy.

BEN: Well, that's the difference of opinion we have over theory.

NED: But your theory turns me into a man from Mars. My theory doesn't do that to you.

BEN: Are you suggesting it was wrong of me to send you into therapy so young? I didn't think you'd stay in it forever.

NED: I didn't think I'd done anything wrong until you sent me into it. Ben, you know you mean more to me than anyone else in the world; you always have. Although I think

I've finally found someone I like... Don't you understand?

BEN: No, I don't understand.

NED: You've got to say it. I'm the same as you. Just say it. Say it!

BEN: No, you're not. I can't say it.

NED: (*He is heartbroken.*) Every time I lose this fight it hurts more. I don't want to have lunch. I'll see you. (*He starts out.*)

BEN: Come on, lemon, I still love you. Sarah loves you. Our children. Our cat. Our dog...

NED: You think this is a joke!

BEN: (*Angry.*) You have my love and you have my legal advice and my financial supervision. I can't give you the courage to stand up and say to me that you don't give a good healthy fuck what I think. Please stop trying to wring some admission of guilt out of me. I am truly happy that you've met someone. It's about time. And I'm sorry your friends are dying...

NED: If you're so sorry, join our honorary board and say you're sorry out loud!

BEN: My agreeing you were born just like I was born is not going to help save your dying friends.

NED: Funny—that's exactly what I think will help save my dying friends.

BEN: Ned—you can be gay and you can be proud no matter what I think. Everybody is oppressed by somebody else in some form or another. Some of us learn how to fight back, with or without the help of others, despite their opinions, even those closest to us. And judging from this mess your friends are in, it's imperative that you stand up and fight to be prouder than ever.

NED: Can't you see that I'm trying to do that? Can't your perverse ego proclaiming its superiority see that I'm trying to be proud? You can only find room to call yourself normal.

BEN: You make me sound like I'm the enemy.

NED: I'm beginning to think that you and your straight world are our enemy. I am furious with you, and with myself and with every goddamned doctor who ever told me I'm sick and interfered with my loving a man. I'm trying to understand why nobody wants to hear we're dying, why nobody wants to help, why my own brother doesn't want to help. Two million dollars—for a house! We can't even get twenty-nine cents from the city. You still think I'm sick, and I simply cannot allow that any longer. I will not speak to you again until you accept me as your equal. Your healthy equal. Your brother! (*He runs out.*)

# Scene 7

NED's *apartment*. FELIX, *working on an article, is spread out on the floor with books, note pad, comforter, and pillows.* NED *enters, eating from a pint of ice cream.*

NED: At the rate I'm going, no one in this city will be talking to me in about three more weeks. I had another fight with Bruce today. I slammed the phone down on him. I don't know why I do that—I'm never finished saying what I want to, so I just have to call him back, during which I inevitably work myself up into another frenzy and hang up on him again. That poor man doesn't know what to do with me. I don't think people like me work at Citibank.

FELIX:   Why can't you see what an ordinary guy Bruce is? I know you think he has hidden qualities, if you just give him plant food he'll grow into the fighter you are. He can't. All he's got is a lot of good looking Pendleton shirts.

NED:   I know there are better ways to handle him. I just can't seem to. This epidemic is killing friendships, too. I can't even talk to my own brother. Why doesn't he call me?

FELIX:   There's the phone.

NED:   Why do I always have to do the running back?

FELIX:   All you ever eat is desserts.

NED:   Sugar is the most important thing in my life. All the rest is just to stay alive.

FELIX:   What was the fight about?

NED:   Which fight?

FELIX:   Bruce.

NED:   Pick a subject.

FELIX:   How many do you know now?

NED:   Forty...dead. That's too many for one person to know. Curt Morgan, this guy I went to Yale with, just died.

FELIX:   Emerick Nolan—he gave me my first job on the *Washington Post*.

NED:   Bruce is getting paranoid: now his lover, Albert, isn't feeling well. Bruce is afraid he's giving it to everyone.

FELIX:   Maybe it isn't paranoia. Maybe what we do with our lovers is what we should be thinking about most of all.

(*The phone rings.* NED *answers it.*)

NED:   Hello. Hold on. (*Locating some pages and reading from them into the phone.*) "It is no secret that I consider the Mayor to be, along with the *Times*, the biggest enemy gay men and women must contend with in New York. Until the day I die I will never forgive this newspaper and this Mayor for ignoring this epidemic that is killing so many of my friends. If..." All right, here's the end. "And every gay man who refuses to come forward now and fight to save his own life is truly helping to kill the rest of us. How many of us have to die before you get scared off your ass and into action?" ... Thank *you.* (*He hangs up.*) I hear it's becoming known as the Ned Weeks School of Outrage.

FELIX:   Who was that?

NED:   Felix, I'm orchestrating this really well. I know I am. We have over six hundred volunteers now. I've got us mentioned in *Time*, *Newsweek*, the evening news on all three networks, both local and national, English and French and Canadian and Australian TV, all the New York area papers except the *Times* and the *Voice*...

FELIX:   You're doing great.

NED:   But they don't support me! Bruce ... this fucking board of directors we put together, all friends of mine—every single one of them yelled at me for two solid hours last night. They think I'm creating a panic, I'm using it to make myself into a celebrity—not one of them will appear on TV or be interviewed, so I do it all by default; so now I'm accused of being self-serving, as if it's fun getting slugged on the subway.

FELIX:   They're beginning to get really frightened. You are becoming a leader. And you love to fight.

NED:   What? I love it?

FELIX:   Yes!

NED:   I love to fight? *Moi?*

FELIX:   Yes, you do, and you're having a wonderful time.

NED:   Yes, I am. (*Meaning* FELIX.)

FELIX:   I did speak to one of our science reporters today.

NED:   (*Delighted.*) Felix! What did he say?

FELIX:   He's gay, too, and afraid they'll find out. Don't yell at me! Ned, I tried. All those shrinks, they must have done something right to you.

NED:   (*Giving* FELIX *a kiss with each name.*) Dr. Malev, Dr. Ritvo, Dr. Gillespie, Dr. Greenacre, Dr. Harkavy, Dr. Klagsbrun, Dr. Donadello, Dr. Levy... I have only one question now: why did it have to take so long?

FELIX:   You think it's them, do you?

NED:   Dr.—I can't remember which one—said it would finally happen. Someone I couldn't scare away would finally show up.

FELIX:   At the baths, why didn't you tell me you were a writer?

NED:   Why didn't you tell me you worked for the *Times?* That I would have remembered.

FELIX:   If I had told you what I did, would you have seen me again?

NED:   Absolutely.

FELIX:   You slut!

NED: Felix, we weren't ready then. If I had it, would you leave me?

FELIX: I don't know. Would you, if I did?

NED: No.

FELIX: How do you know?

NED: I just know. You had to have had my mother. She was a dedicated full-time social worker for the Red Cross—she put me to work on the Bloodmobile when I was eight. She was always getting an award for being best bloodcatcher or something. She's eighty now—touring China. I don't think I'm programmed any other way.

FELIX: I have something to tell you.

NED: You're pregnant.

FELIX: I was married once.

NED: Does that make me the other woman?

FELIX: I thought I was supposed to be straight. She said I had been unfair to her, which I had been. I have a son.

NED: You have a son?

FELIX: She won't let me see him.

NED: You can't see your own son? But didn't you fight? That means you're ashamed. So he will be, too.

FELIX: That's why I didn't tell you before. And who says I didn't fight! What happens to someone who cannot be as strong as you want them to be?

NED: Felix, weakness terrifies me. It scares the shit out of me. My father was weak and I'm afraid I'll be like him. His life didn't stand for anything, and then it was over. So I fight. Constantly. And if I can do it, I can't understand why everybody else can't do it, too. Okay?

FELIX:   Okay. (*He pulls off one of his socks and shows* NED *a purple spot on his foot*.) It keeps getting bigger and bigger, Neddie, and it doesn't go away.

**End of Act One**

# ACT TWO

## Scene 8

EMMA's *apartment.* EMMA *and* NED *are having brunch. She uses a nonmotorized, i.e., regular, wheelchair.*

NED: You look very pretty.

EMMA: Thank you.

NED: Where's your cat?

EMMA: Under my bed. She's afraid of you.

NED: Do you think being Jewish makes you always hungry?

EMMA: I'm not Jewish.

NED: You're not?

EMMA: I'm German.

NED: Everyone thinks you're Jewish.

EMMA: I know. In medicine that helps.

NED: How many of us do you think already have the virus in our system?

EMMA: In this city—easily over half of all gay men.

NED: So we're just walking time bombs—waiting for whatever it is that sets us off.

EMMA: Yes. And before a vaccine can be discovered almost

**77**

every gay man will have been exposed. Ned, your organization is worthless! I went up and down Christopher Street last night and all I saw was guys going in the bars alone and coming out with somebody. And outside the baths, all I saw was lines of guys going in. And what is this stupid publication you finally put out? (*She holds up a pamphlet.*) After all we've talked about? You leave too much margin for intelligence. Why aren't you telling them, bluntly, stop! Every day you don't tell them, more people infect each other.

NED:    Don't lecture me. I'm on your side. Remember?

EMMA:    Don't be on my side! I don't need you on my side. Make your side shape up. I've seen 238 cases—me: one doctor. You make it sound like there's nothing worse going around than measles.

NED:    They wouldn't print what I wrote. Again.

EMMA:    What do you mean "they"? Who's they? I thought you and Bruce were the leaders.

NED:    Now we've got a board. You need a board of directors when you become tax-exempt. It was a pain in the ass finding anyone to serve on it at all! I called every prominent gay man I could get to. Forget it! Finally, what we put together turns out to be a bunch as timid as Bruce. And every time Bruce doesn't agree with me, he puts it to a board vote.

EMMA:    And you lose.

NED:    (*Nods.*) Bruce is in the closet; Mickey works for the Health Department; he starts shaking every time I criticize them—they won't even put out leaflets listing all the symptoms; Richard, Dick, and Lennie owe their jobs somehow to the Mayor; Dan is a schoolteacher; we're not allowed to say his last name out loud; the rest are just a bunch of disco dumbies. I warned you this was not a community that has its best interests at heart.

EMMA: But this is death.

NED: And the board doesn't want any sex recommendations at all. No passing along anything that isn't a hundred percent certain.

EMMA: You must tell them that's wrong! Nothing is a hundred percent certain in science, so you won't be saying anything.

NED: I think that's the general idea.

EMMA: Then why did you bother to start an organization at all?

NED: Now they've decided they only want to take care of patients—crisis counseling, support groups, home attendants...I know that's important, too. But I thought I was starting with a bunch of Ralph Naders and Green Berets, and the first instant they have to take a stand on a political issue and fight, almost in front of my eyes they turn into a bunch of nurses' aides.

EMMA: You've got to warn the living, protect the healthy, help them keep on living. I'll take care of the dying.

NED: They keep yelling at me that I can't expect an entire world to suddenly stop making love. And now I've got to tell them there's absolutely no such thing as safe sex...

EMMA: I don't consider going to the baths and promiscuous sex making love. I consider it the equivalent of eating junk food, and you can lay off it for a while. And, yes, I do expect it, and you get them to come sit in my office any day of the week and they'd expect it, too. Get a VCR, rent a porn film, and use your hands!

NED: Why are you yelling at me for what I'm not doing?

What the fuck is your side doing? Where's the goddamned AMA in all of this? The government has not started one single test tube of research. Where's the board of directors of your very own hospital? You have so many patients you haven't got rooms for them, and you've got to make Felix well ... So what am I yelling at you for?

EMMA:   Who's Felix? Who is Felix?

NED:   I introduced you to him at that Health Forum you spoke at.

EMMA:   You've taken a lover?

NED:   We live together. Emma, I've never been so much in love in my life. I've never been in love. Late Friday night he showed me this purple spot on the bottom of his foot. Maybe it isn't it. Maybe it's some sort of something else. It could be, couldn't it? Maybe I'm overreacting. There's so much death around. Can you see him tomorrow? I know you're booked up for weeks. But could you?

EMMA:   Tell him to call me first thing tomorrow. Seven-thirty. I'll fit him in.

NED:   Thank you.

EMMA:   God damn you!

NED:   I know I should have told you.

EMMA:   What's done is done.

NED:   What are we supposed to do—be with nobody ever? Well, it's not as easy as you might think. (*She wheels herself directly in front of him.*) Oh, Emma, I'm so sorry.

EMMA:   Don't be. Polio is a virus, too. I caught it three months before the Salk vaccine was announced. Nobody gets polio anymore.

NED:   Were you in an iron lung?

EMMA: For a while. But I graduated from college and from medical school first in my class. They were terrified of me. The holy terror in the wheelchair. Still are. I scare the shit out of people.

NED: I think I do, too.

EMMA: Learn how to use it. It can be very useful. Don't need everybody's love and approval. (*He embraces her impulsively; she comforts him.*) You've got to get out there on the line more than ever now.

NED: We finally have a meeting at City Hall tomorrow.

EMMA: Good. You take care of the city—I'll take care of Felix.

NED: I'm afraid to be with him; I'm afraid to be without him; I'm afraid the cure won't come in time; I'm afraid of my anger; I'm a terrible leader and a useless lover...

(*He holds on to her again. Then he kisses her, breaks away from her, grabs his coat, and leaves. Emma is alone.*)

# Scene 9

*A meeting room in City Hall. It's in a basement, windowless, dusty, a room that's hardly ever used.* NED *and* BRUCE *wait impatiently; they have been fighting.* BRUCE *wears a suit, having come from his office, with his attaché case. Both wear overcoats.*

NED: How dare they do this to us?

BRUCE:  It's one-thirty. Maybe he's not going to show up. Why don't we just leave?

NED:  Keeping us down here in some basement room that hasn't been used in years. What contempt!

BRUCE:  I'm sorry I let you talk me into coming here. It's not the city's responsibility to take care of us. That's why New York went broke.

NED:  What we're asking for doesn't cost the city a dime: let us meet with the mayor; let him declare an emergency; have him put pressure on Washington for money for research; have him get the *Times* to write about us.

BRUCE:  The Mayor's not going to help. Besides, if we get too political, we'll lose our tax-exempt status. That's what the lawyer in your brother's office said.

NED:  You don't think the American Cancer Society, the Salvation Army, any charity you can think of, isn't somehow political, isn't putting pressure on somebody somewhere? The Catholic Church? We should be riding herd on the CDC in Atlanta—they deny it's happening in straight people, when it is. We could organize boycotts...

BRUCE:  Boycotts? What in the world is there to boycott?

NED:  Have you been following this Tylenol scare? In three months there have been seven deaths, and the *Times* has written fifty-four articles. The month of October alone they ran one article every single day. Four of them were on the front page. For us—in seventeen months they've written seven puny inside articles. And we have a thousand cases!

BRUCE:  So?

NED:  So the *Times* won't write about us, why should we read it?

BRUCE: I read it every morning. The next thing you'll say is we should stop shopping at Bloomingdale's.

NED: We should picket the White House!

BRUCE: Brilliant.

NED: Don't you have any vision of what we could become? A powerful national organization effecting change! Bruce, you must have been a fighter once. When you were a Green Beret, did you kill people?

BRUCE: A couple of times.

NED: Did you like being a soldier?

BRUCE: I loved it.

NED: Then why did you quit?

BRUCE: I didn't quit! I just don't like being earmarked gay.

NED: Bruce, what are you doing in this organization?

BRUCE: There are a lot of sick people out there that need our help.

NED: There are going to be a lot more sick people out there if we don't get our act together. Did you give up combat completely?

BRUCE: Don't you fucking talk to me about combat! I just fight different from you.

NED: I haven't seen your way yet.

BRUCE: Oh, you haven't? Where have you been?

NED: Bruce, Albert may be dying. Why doesn't that alone make you want to fight harder?

BRUCE: Get off my back!

NED: Get off your ass!

(TOMMY *enters*.)

TOMMY: Wonderful—we finally get a meeting with the Mayor's assistant and you two are having another fight.

BRUCE: I didn't have the fight, he had the fight. It's always Ned who has the fight.

TOMMY: Where the hell are we? What kind of tomb is this they put us in? Don't they want us to be seen above ground? Where is he? I'm an hour late.

NED: An hour and a half. And where's Mickey?

TOMMY: Not with me, lambchop. I've been up at Bellevue. I put a sweet dying child together with his momma. They hadn't seen each other for fifteen years and he'd never told her he was gay, so he didn't want to see her now. He's been refusing to see her for weeks and he was furious with me when I waltzed in with her and... It was a real weeper, Momma holding her son, and he's dead now. There are going to be a lot of mommas flying into town not understanding why their sons have suddenly upped and died from "pneumonia." You two've been barking at each other for an hour and a half? My, my.

BRUCE: Tommy, he makes me so mad.

NED: CBS called. They want our president to go on Dan Rather. He won't do it. They don't want anybody else.

BRUCE: I can't go on national television!

NED: Then you shouldn't be our president! Tommy, look at that. Imagine what a fantastic impression he would make on the whole country, speaking out for something gay. You're the kind of role model we need, not those drag queens from San Francisco who shove their faces in front of every camera they see.

BRUCE:  You want to pay me my salary and my pension and my health insurance, I'll go on TV.

TOMMY:  Both of you, stop it. Can't you see we need both your points of view? Ned plays the bad cop and Bruce plays the good cop; every successful corporation works that way. You're both our leaders and we need you both desperately.

NED:  Tommy, how is not going on national TV playing good cop?

(MICKEY *enters*.)

MICKEY:  I couldn't get out of work. I was afraid you'd be finished by now.

BRUCE:  (*To* MICKEY.) Did you see his latest *Native* article?

MICKEY:  Another one?

NED:  What's so awful about what I said? It's the truth.

BRUCE:  But it's how you say it!

MICKEY:  What'd you say?

NED:  I said we're all cowards! I said rich gays will give thousands to straight charities before they'll give us a dime. I said it is appalling that some twenty million men and women don't have one single lobbyist in Washington. How do we expect to achieve anything, ever, at all, by immaculate conception? I said the gay leaders who created this sexual-liberation philosophy in the first place have been the death of us. Mickey, why didn't you guys fight for the right to get married instead of the right to legitimize promiscuity?

MICKEY:  We did!

TOMMY:  I get your drift.

MICKEY:  Sure you didn't leave anybody out?

NED: I said it's all our fault, every one of us...

(HIRAM KEEBLER, *the Mayor's assistant, enters, and* NED *carries on without a break*.)

...and you are an hour and forty-five minutes late, so why'd you bother to come at all?

BRUCE: Ned!

HIRAM: I presume I am at last having the pleasure of meeting Mr. Weeks' lilting telephone voice face to face. (*Shaking hands all around*.) I'm truly sorry I'm late.

MICKEY: (*Shaking hands*.) Michael Marcus.

HIRAM: I'm Hiram Keebler.

TOMMY: Are you related to the folks who make the crackers? Tommy Boatwright.

BRUCE: Bruce Niles.

HIRAM: The Mayor wants you to know how much he cares and how impressed he is with your superb efforts to shoulder your own responsibility.

BRUCE: Thank you.

NED: Our responsibility? Everything we're doing is stuff you should be doing. And we need help.

TOMMY: What Mr. Weeks is trying to say, sir, is that, well, we are truly swamped. We're now fielding over five hundred calls a week on our emergency hot line, people everywhere are desperate for information, which, quite frankly, the city should be providing, but isn't. We're visiting over one hundred patients each week in hospitals and homes and...

BRUCE: Sir, one thing you could help us with is office space. We're presently in one small room, and at least one hundred people come in and out every day and... no one will rent to us because of what we do and who we are.

HIRAM: That's illegal discrimination.

TOMMY: We believe we know that to be true, sir.

MICKEY: (*Nervously speaking up.*) Mr. Keebler, sir, it is not illegal to discriminate against homosexuals.

NED: We have been trying to see the mayor for fourteen months. It has taken us one year just to get this meeting with you and you are an hour and forty-five minutes late. Have you told the mayor there's an epidemic going on?

HIRAM: I can't tell him that!

NED: Why not?

HIRAM: Because it isn't true.

BRUCE: Yes, sir, it is.

HIRAM: Who said so?

TOMMY: The government.

HIRAM: Which government? Our government?

NED: No! Russia's government!

HIRAM: Since when?

MICKEY: The Centers for Disease Control in Atlanta declared it.

TOMMY: Seventeen months ago.

NED: How could you not know that?

HIRAM: Well, you can't expect us to concern ourselves with every little outbreak those boys come up with. And could you please reduce the level of your hysteria?

NED: Certainly. San Francisco, LA, Miami, Boston, Chicago, Washington, Denver, Houston, Seattle, Dallas—all now report cases. It's cropping up in Paris, London, Germany, Canada. But New York City, our home, the city you are pledged to protect, has over half of everything: half the one thousand cases, half the dead. Two hundred and fifty-six dead. And I know forty of them. And I don't want to know any more. And you can't not know any of this! Now—when can we see the mayor? Fourteen months is a long time to be out to lunch!

HIRAM: Now wait a minute!

NED: No, you wait a minute. We can't. Time is not on our side. If you won't take word to the Mayor, what do we do? How do we get it to him? Hire a hunky hustler and send him up to Gracie Mansion with our plea tattooed on his cock?

HIRAM: The Mayor is not gay!

TOMMY: Oh, come on, Blanche!

BRUCE: Tommy!

HIRAM: Now you listen to me! Of course we're aware of those figures. And before you open your big mouth again, I would like to offer you a little piece of advice. Bad-mouthing the Mayor is the best way I know to not get his attention.

NED: We're not getting it now, so what have we got to lose?

BRUCE: Ned!

NED: Bruce, you just heard him. Hiram here just said they're aware of the figures. And they're still not doing anything. I was worried before that they were just stupid and blind. Great! Now we get to worry about them being repressive and downright dangerous.

BRUCE: Ned! I'm sorry, sir, but we've been under a great deal of strain.

NED: (*To* BRUCE.) Don't you ever apologize for me again. (*To* HIRAM.) How dare you choose who will live and who will die!

HIRAM:  Now, listen: don't you think I want to help you? (*Confidentially.*) I have a friend who's dying from this in VA Hospital right this very minute.

NED:  Then why...?

HIRAM:  Because it's tricky, can't you see that? It's very tricky.

NED:  Tricky, shit! There are a million gay people in New York. A million and one, counting you. That's a lot of votes. Our organization started with six men. We now have over six hundred active volunteers and a mailing list of ten thousand.

HIRAM:  Six hundred? You think the mayor worries about six hundred? A fire goes out in a school furnace on the West Side between Seventy-second and Ninety-sixth streets, I get three thousand phone calls. In one day! You know what I'm talking about?

NED:  Yes.

HIRAM:  If so many of you are so upset about what's happening, why do I only hear from this loudmouth?

NED:  That's a very good question.

HIRAM:  Okay—there are half a million gay men in our area. Five hundred and nine cases doesn't seem so high, considering how many of us—I mean, of you!—there are.

NED:  This is bullshit!

BRUCE:  Ned! Let me take it. Sir—

HIRAM:  Hiram, please. You are?

BRUCE:  I'm Bruce Niles. I'm the president.

HIRAM:  You're the president? What does that make Mr. Weeks here?

BRUCE:  He's one of the founders.

NED:   But we work together jointly.

HIRAM:   Oh, you do?

NED:   Yes, we do.

HIRAM:   Carry on, Mr. Niles.

BRUCE:   Look, we realize things are tricky, but—

HIRAM:   (*Cutting him off.*) Yes, it is. And the Mayor feels there is no need to declare any kind of emergency. That only gets people excited. And we simply can't give you office space. We're not in the free-giveaway business.

BRUCE:   We don't want it for free. We will pay for it.

HIRAM:   I repeat, I think—that is, the mayor thinks you guys are overreacting.

NED:   You tell that cocksucker that he's a selfish, heartless, son of a bitch!

HIRAM:   You are now heading for real trouble! Do you think you can barge in here and call us names? (*To* MICKEY.) You are Michael L. Marcus. You hold an unsecured job with the City Department of Health. I'd watch my step if I were you. You got yourself quite a handful here. You might consider putting him in a cage in the zoo. That I think I can arrange with the Mayor. I'd watch out for my friends here if I were you. The Mayor won't have it! (*Exits.*)

MICKEY:   I don't believe this just happened.

NED:   Mickey, I'm on the *Today Show* tomorrow and I'm going to say the Mayor is threatening your job if we don't shut up.

MICKEY:   The *Today Show*! You're going to do what?!

BRUCE:   You can't do that!

NED:   Of course I can: he just did.

BRUCE:   God damn it, Ned!

NED:   We're being treated like shit. (*He yells after them as they pick up their things and leave.*) And we're allowing it. And until we force them to treat us otherwise, we get exactly what we deserve. Politicians understand only one thing— pressure! You heard him—him and his three thousand West Side phone calls. We're not yelling loud enough! Bruce, for a Green Beret, you're an awful sissy! (*He is all alone.*)

# Scene 10

EMMA's *office.* FELIX *sits on the examining table, wearing a white hospital gown.* EMMA *sits facing him.*

FELIX:   So it is... it.

EMMA:   Yes.

FELIX:   There's not a little bit of doubt in your mind? You don't want to call in Christiaan Barnard?

EMMA:   I'm sorry. I still don't know how to tell people. They don't teach acting in medical school.

FELIX:   Aren't you worried about contagion? I mean, I assume I am about to become a leper.

EMMA:   Well, I'm still here.

FELIX:   Do you think they'll find a cure before I... How strange that sounds when you say it out loud for the first time.

EMMA:   We're trying. But we're poor. Uncle Sam is the only place these days that can afford the kind of research that's needed, and so far we've not even had the courtesy of a reply from our numerous requests to him. You guys are still not making enough noise.

FELIX:   That's Ned's department in our family. I'm not feeling too political at the moment.

EMMA:   I'd like to try a treatment of several chemotherapies used together. It's milder than others. You're an early case.

FELIX:   I assume that's hopeful.

EMMA:   It's always better early.

FELIX:   It also takes longer until you die.

EMMA:   Yes. You can look at it that way.

FELIX:   Do you want a second opinion?

EMMA:   Feel free. But I'll say this about my fellow hospitals, which I shouldn't: you won't get particularly good care anywhere, maybe not even here. At... I'll call it Hospital A, you'll come under a group of mad scientists, research fanatics, who will try almost anything and if you die you die. You'll rarely see the same doctor twice; you'll just be a statistic for their computer—which they won't share with anyone else, by the way; there's not much sharing going on, never is—you'll be a true guinea pig. At Hospital B, they decided they really didn't want to get involved with this, it's too messy, and they're right, so you'll be overlooked by the least informed of doctors. C is like the *New York Times* and our friends everywhere: square, righteous, superior, and embarrassed by this disease and this entire epidemic. D is Catholic. E is Jewish. F is... Why am I telling you this? I must be insane. But the situation is insane.

FELIX:   I guess we better get started.

EMMA: We have. You'll come to me once a week. There are going to be a lot of tests, a lot of blood tests, a lot of waiting. My secretary will give you a long list of dos and don'ts. Now, Felix, you understand your body no longer has any effective mechanism for fighting off anything?

FELIX: I'm going to be all right, you know.

EMMA: Good. That's the right attitude.

FELIX: No, I'm going to be the one who kicks it. I've always been lucky.

EMMA: Good.

FELIX: I guess everyone says that. Well, I'm going to be the one. I wanted a job on the *Times*, I got it. I wanted Ned ... Have I given it to Ned?

EMMA: I don't know.

FELIX: Can he catch it from me now?

EMMA: We just don't know.

FELIX: Did he give it to me?

EMMA: Only one out of a hundred adults infected with the polio virus gets it; virtually everybody infected with rabies dies. One person has a cold, hepatitis—sometimes the partner catches it, sometimes not. I don't think we'll ever know why.

FELIX: No more making love?

EMMA: Right.

FELIX: Some gay doctors are saying it's okay if you use rubbers.

EMMA: I know they are.

FELIX: Can we kiss?

EMMA: I don't know.

FELIX:   (*After a long pause.*) I want my mother.

EMMA:   Where is she?

FELIX:   She's dead. We never got along anyway.

EMMA:   I'm going to do my damnedest, Felix. (*She starts to leave.*)

FELIX:   Hey, Doc...I'll bet you say that to all the boys.

———————————————

# Scene 11

*A small, crowded office. Many phones are ringing.* TOMMY *is on two at once;* MICKY, *going crazy, is on another, trying to understand and hear in the din; and* GRADY, *a volunteer, also on a phone, is trying to pass papers and information to either.*

MICKEY:   Hello. Just a moment. It's another theory call. Okay, go ahead. Uranus...? (*Writing it down.*)

GRADY:   Whose asshole you talking about, Mickey?

MICKEY:   Grady!

TOMMY:   (*To* GRADY.) I thought your friend, little Vinnie, was going to show up today.

MICKEY:   He had to go to the gym.

MICKEY:   (*Reading into the phone what he's written.*) "Mystical electromagnetic fields ruled by the planet Uranus?" Yes, well, we'll certainly keep that in mind. Thank you for calling and sharing that with us.

GRADY:   Harry's in a pay phone at the post office.

MICKEY:   Get a number, we'll call him back.

GRADY:   (*Into phone.*) Give me the number, I'll call you back.

TOMMY:   (*Into one phone.*) Philip, can you hold on? (Into second phone.) Graciella, you tell Señor Hiram I've been holding for *diez minutos* and he called me. *Sí, sí!* (*Into first phone.*) You know where St. Vincent's is? You get your ass there fast! I'll send you a crisis counselor later today. I know you're scared, honey, but just get there.

(GRADY *hands* MICKEY *Harry's number.* TOMMY *has hung up one phone.*)

MICKEY:   Well, call him back!

(BRUCE *comes in, dressed as from the office, with his attaché case.*)

TOMMY:   Mickey, do we have a crisis counselor we can send to St. V's around six o'clock?

MICKEY:   (*Consulting a chart on a wall.*) No.

TOMMY:   Shit. (*To* BRUCE.) Hi, Bossman.

BRUCE:   (*Answering a ringing phone.*) Hello. How ya doin'! (*To the room.*) It's Kessler in San Francisco.

GRADY:   (*Into his phone.*) Louder, Harry! It's a madhouse. None of the volunteers showed up.

MICKEY:   (*Busying himself with paperwork.*) Mystical?!

GRADY:   (*On his phone.*) Oh, dear.

BRUCE:   (*On his.*) No kidding.

GRADY:   Oh, dear!

TOMMY:   (*Picking up a ringing phone.*) Ned's not here yet.

BRUCE:   (*To the room.*) San Francisco's mayor is giving four million dollars to their organization. (*Into phone.*) Well, we still haven't met our mayor. We met with his assistant about four months ago.

TOMMY:  (*To* BRUCE.) Hiram called three days ago and left a message he found some money for us. Try and get him back.

MICKEY:  We need to train some more crisis counselors.

GRADY:  What about me, Mick?

TOMMY:  (*Standing up.*) Okay, get this! The *Times* is finally writing a big story. Twenty months after the epidemic has been declared, the *Times* is finally writing a big story. Word is that Craig Claiborne took someone high up out to lunch and told them they really had to write something, anything.

MICKEY:  Who's writing it?

TOMMY:  Some lady in Baltimore.

MICKEY:  Makes sense. (*His phone rings.*) Hello.

GRADY:  (*Still on his phone.*) Oh, dear.

TOMMY:  Grady, darling, what the fuck are you oh-dearing about?

GRADY:  (*Dropping his bombshell to Bruce.*) Bruce—Harry says the post office won't accept our mailing.

BRUCE:  What! (*Into phone.*) Got to go. (*Slams phone down and grabs* GRADY'S.) Harry, what's the problem?

MICKEY:  (*Into his phone.*) That's awful.

BRUCE:  (*Into his phone.*) They can't do that to us!

TOMMY:  (*Who hadn't heard* GRADY.) What is it now?

GRADY:  Harry went to the post office with the fifty-seven cartons of our new Newsletters—

TOMMY:  Sugar, I sent him there!

GRADY:  Well, they're not going anywhere.

BRUCE:   (*To* TOMMY.) The post office won't accept them because we just used our initials.

TOMMY:   So what?

BRUCE:   In order to get tax-exemption we have to use our full name.

TOMMY:   There is a certain amount of irony in all this, though not right now.

GRADY:   He's double-parked and his volunteers had to go home.

TOMMY:   Grady, dear, would you go help him out.

GRADY:   No.

TOMMY *and* MICKEY:   Grady!

GRADY:   No! Why do I always have to do the garbage stuff?

MICKEY:   Grady!

GRADY:   Give me the phone. (*Into phone*.) Hold on, Harry, I'm coming to help you. (*To* TOMMY.) Give me cab fare.

TOMMY:   Ride the rail, boy.

BRUCE:   (*Into the phone*.) Harry, someone's coming. (*Whispering to* TOMMY.) What's his name?

TOMMY *and* MICKEY: Grady.

(GRADY *exits*.)

BRUCE:   (*Into phone*.) Harry, bring them back. I want to fight this further somewhere. I'm sorry, I know it's a schlepp.

TOMMY:   So this means we either pay full rate or embarrass their mailmen. Sorry, honey, I couldn't resist. (*Into phone*.) Graciella! (*To the room*.) How do you say I've been holding twenty minutes in Spanish? (*Into phone*.) City Hall is an equal-opportunity employer, doesn't that mean you all have to learn English? (*He hangs up*.)

MICKEY:   (*Hanging up.*) That was Atlanta. They're reporting thirty cases a week now nationally.

BRUCE:   Thirty?

TOMMY:   The CDC are filthy liars. What's wrong with those boys? We log forty cases a week in this office alone.

BRUCE:   Forty?

TOMMY:   Forty.

MICKEY:   Thirty.

BRUCE:   (*Trying to decide how to enter this on the wall chart.*) So that's thirty nationally, forty in this office alone.

TOMMY:   You heard what I said. (*Dialing, then into phone.*) Hi. Pick up for us, will you, dears? We need a little rest. Thank you. (*Hangs up.*)

(*There is a long moment of silence, strange now without the ringing phones.* TOMMY *lights a cigarette and sits back.* MICKEY *tries to concentrate on some paperwork.* BRUCE *is at the wall entering figures on charts.*)

BRUCE:   Mickey . . . aren't you supposed to be in Rio?

MICKEY:   Where's Ned?

TOMMY:   He should be here by now.

BRUCE:   I don't want to see him.

MICKEY:   I need to talk to him. I don't want to lose my job because Ned doesn't like sex very much. He's coming on like Jesus Christ, as if he never took a lover himself.

BRUCE:   Rio. Why aren't you in Rio?

MICKEY:   I was in Rio. I'm tired. I need a rest.

BRUCE:   We're all exhausted.

TOMMY:   You're the president; you can't have a rest.

MICKEY:   I work all day for the city writing stuff on breast-feeding versus formula and how to stay calm if you have herpes and I work all night on our Newsletter and my health columns for the *Native* and I can't take it anymore. Now this...

TOMMY:   Take it slowly.

BRUCE:   Now what?

MICKEY:   I was in Rio, Gregory and I are in Rio, we just got there, day before yesterday, I get a phone call, from Hiram's office.

BRUCE:   In Rio?

MICKEY:   I'm told to be at a meeting at his office right away, this morning.

BRUCE:   What kind of meeting? Why didn't you call me and I could have checked it out?

MICKEY:   Because, unfortunately, you are not my boss.

BRUCE:   What kind of meeting?

MICKEY:   I don't know. I get to City Hall, he keeps me waiting forever; finally the Commissioner comes, my boss, and he said I hope you had a nice vacation, and went inside, into Hiram's office; and I waited some more, and the Commissioner comes out and says, Hiram doesn't want to see you anymore. I said, please, sir, then why did he make me come all the way back from Rio? He said, your vacation isn't over? I said, no sir, I was just there one day. I wanted to scream I haven't slept in two days, you dumb fuck! but I didn't. What I said was, sir, does this mean I'm fired? And the Commissioner said, no, I don't think he means that, and he left.

(NED *enters, unnoticed.*)

MICKEY:   Ned's article in the *Native* attacking Hiram came out last week. I love sex! I worship men! I don't think Ned does. I don't think Ned likes himself. I—

NED:   What are you trying to say, Mickey?

MICKEY:   You keep trying to make us say things that we don't want to say! And I don't think we can afford to make so many enemies before we have enough friends.

NED:   We'll never have enough friends. We have to accept that. And why does what I say mean I don't like myself? Why is anything I'm saying compared to anything but common sense? When are we going to have this out once and for all? How many cases a week now?

MICKEY:   Thirty . . . forty . . .

NED:   Reinhard dead, Craig dead, Albert sick, Felix not getting any better . . . Richie Faro just died.

MICKEY:   Richie!

NED:   That guy Ray Schwartz just committed suicide. Terry's calling all his friends from under his oxygen tent to say good-bye. Soon we're going to be blamed for not doing anything to help ourselves. When are we going to admit we might be spreading this? We have simply fucked ourselves silly for years and years, and sometimes we've done it in the filthiest places.

TOMMY:   Some of us have never been to places like that, Ned.

NED:   Well, good for you, Tommy. Maybe you haven't, but others you've been with have, so what's the difference?

TOMMY:   (*Holding up his cigarette.*) It's my right to kill myself.

NED:   But it is not your right to kill me. This is not a civil-rights issue, this is a contagion issue.

BRUCE: We don't know that yet, and until they discover the virus, we're not certain where this is coming from.

NED: We know enough to cool it for a while! And save lives while we do. All it takes is one wrong fuck. That's not promiscuity—that's bad luck.

TOMMY: All right, so it's back to kissing and cuddling and waiting around for Mr. Right—who could be Mr. Wrong. Maybe if they'd let us get married to begin with none of this would have happened at all. I think I'll call Dr. Ruth.

MICKEY: Will you please stop!

TOMMY: Mick, are you all right?

MICKEY: I don't think so.

TOMMY: What's wrong? Tell Tommy.

MICKEY: Why can't they find the virus?

TOMMY: It takes time.

MICKEY: I can't take any more theories. I've written a column about every single one of them. Repeated infection by a virus, new appearance by a dormant virus, single virus, new virus, old virus, multivirus, partial virus, latent virus, mutant virus, retrovirus...

TOMMY: Take it easy, honey.

MICKEY: And we mustn't forget fucking, sucking, kissing, blood, voodoo, drugs, poppers, needles, Africa, Haiti, Cuba, blacks, amebas, pigs, mosquitoes, monkeys, Uranus!... What if it isn't any of them?

TOMMY: I don't know.

MICKEY: What if it's something out of the blue? The Great Plague of London was caused by polluted drinking water from a pump nobody noticed. Maybe it's a genetic predisposition, or the theory of the herd—only so many of us will get it and then the pool's used up. What if it's monogamy? Bruce, you and I could actually be worse off because of constant bombardment of the virus from a single source— our own lovers! Maybe guys who go to the baths regularly have built up the best immunity! I don't know what to tell anybody. And everybody asks *me*. I don't know—who's right? I don't know—who's wrong? I feel so inadequate! How can we tell people to stop when it might turn out to be caused by—I don't know!

BRUCE:   That's exactly how I feel.

MICKEY:   And Ned keeps calling the Mayor a prick and Hiram a prick and the Commissioner a prick and the President and the *New York Times*, and that's the entire political structure of the entire United States! When are you going to stop your eternal name-calling at every person you see?

BRUCE:   That's exactly how I feel.

MICKEY:   But maybe he's right! And that scares me, too. Neddie, you scare me.

TOMMY:   If I were you, I'd get back on that plane to Gregory and Rio immediately.

MICKEY:   Who's going to pay my fare? And now my job, I don't make much, but it's enough to let me help out here. Where are all the gay Rockefellers? Do you think the President really wants this to happen? Do you think the CIA really has unleashed germ warfare to kill off all the queers Jerry Falwell doesn't want? Why should they help us; we're actually cooperating with them by dying?

NED:   Mickey, try and hold on.

MICKEY:   To what? I used to love my country. The *Native* received an anonymous letter describing top-secret Defense

Department experiments at Fort Detrick, Maryland, that have produced a virus that can destroy the immune system. Its code name is Firm Hand. They started testing in 1978—on a group of gays. I never used to believe shit like this before. They are going to persecute us! Cancel our health insurance. Test our blood to see if we're pure. Lock us up. Stone us in the streets. (*To* NED.) And you think I am killing people?

NED:  Mickey, that is not what I—

MICKEY:  Yes, you do! I know you do! I've spent fifteen years of my life fighting for our right to be free and make love whenever, wherever . . . And you're telling me that all those years of what being gay stood for is wrong . . . and I'm a murderer. We have been so oppressed! Don't you remember how it was? Can't you see how important it is for us to love openly, without hiding and without guilt? We were a bunch of funny-looking fellows who grew up in sheer misery and one day we fell into the orgy rooms and we thought we'd found heaven. And we would teach the world how wonderful heaven can be. We would lead the way. We would be good for something new. Can't you see that? Can't you?

TOMMY:  I see that. I do, Mickey. Come on—I'm taking you home now.

MICKEY:  When I left Hiram's office I went to the top of the Empire State Building to jump off.

TOMMY:  (*Going to get* MICKEY's *coat.*) Mickey, I'm taking you home right now! Let's go.

MICKEY:  You can jump off from there if no one is looking. Ned, I'm not a murderer. All my life I've been hated. For one reason or another. For being short. For being Jewish. Jerry Falwell mails out millions of pictures of two men kissing as if that was the most awful sight you could see. Tell everybody we were wrong. And I'm sorry. Someday someone will come along and put the knife in you and say everything you fought for all this time is...shit! (*He has made a furious, running lunge for* NED, *but* TOMMY *catches him and cradles him in his arms.*)

BRUCE: Need any help?

TOMMY: Get my coat. (*To* MICKEY.) You're just a little tired, that's all, a little bit yelled out. We've got a lot of different styles that don't quite mesh. We've got ourselves a lot of bereavement overload. Tommy's taking you home.

MICKEY: No, don't take me home. I'm afraid I might do something. Take me to St. Vincent's. I'm just afraid.

TOMMY: I'll take you wherever you want to go. (*To* BRUCE *and* NED.) Okay, you two, no more apologizing and no more fucking excuses. You two better start accommodating and talking to each other now. Or we're in big trouble.

MICKEY: We're the fighters, aren't we?

TOMMY: You bet, sweetness. And you're a hero. Whether you know it or not. You're our first hero.

(TOMMY *and* MICKEY *leave. There is a long moment of silence.*)

NED: We're all going to go crazy, living this epidemic every minute, while the rest of the world goes on out there, all around us, as if nothing is happening, going on with their own lives and not knowing what it's like, what we're going through. We're living through war, but where they're living it's peacetime, and we're all in the same country.

BRUCE: Do you want to be president?

NED: I just want Felix to live. (*A phone on* TOMMY's *desk rings.*) Hello. Hiram, old buddy, how they hanging? I want to talk to you, too. (*He listens, then hangs up softly.*) Tommy's right. All yelled out. You ready?

BRUCE:   Yes.

NED:   The Mayor has found a secret little fund for giving away money. But we're not allowed to tell anyone where we got it. If word gets out we've told, we won't get it.

BRUCE:   How much?

NED:   Nine thousand dollars.

BRUCE:   Ned, Albert is dead.

NED:   Oh, no.

BRUCE:   What's today?

NED:   Wednesday.

BRUCE:   He's been dead a week.

NED:   I didn't know he was so close.

BRUCE:   No one did. He wouldn't tell anyone. Do you know why? Because of me. Because he knows I'm so scared I'm some sort of carrier. This makes three people I've been with who are dead. I went to Emma and I begged her: please test me somehow, please tell me if I'm giving this to people. And she said she couldn't, there isn't any way they can find out anything because they still don't know what they're looking for. Albert, I think I loved him best of all, and he went so fast. His mother wanted him back in Phoenix before he died, this was last week when it was obvious, so I get permission from Emma and bundle him all up and take him to the plane in an ambulance. The pilot wouldn't take off and I refused to leave the plane—you would have been proud of me—so finally they get another pilot. Then, after we take off, Albert loses his mind, not recognizing me, not knowing where he is or that he's going home, and then, right there, on the plane, he becomes...incontinent. He starts doing it in his pants and all over the seat; shit, piss, everything. I pulled down my suitcase and yanked out whatever clothes were in there and I start mopping him up as best I can, and all these people are staring at us and moving away in droves and...I ram all these clothes back in the suitcase and I sit there holding his hand, saying, "Albert, please, no more, hold it in, man, I beg you, just for us, for Bruce and Albert." And when we got to Phoenix, there's a police van waiting for us and all the police are in complete protective rubber clothing, they looked like fucking astronauts, and by the time we got to the hospital where his mother had fixed up his room real nice, Albert was dead.

(NED *starts toward him.*)

Wait. It gets worse. The hospital doctors refused to examine him to put a cause of death on the death certificate, and without a death certificate the undertakers wouldn't take him away, and neither would the police. Finally, some orderly comes in and stuffs Albert in a heavy-duty Glad Bag and motions us with his finger to follow and he puts him out in the back alley with the garbage. He says, "Hey, man. See what a big favor I've done for you, I got him out, I want fifty bucks." I paid him and then his mother and I carried the bag to her car and we finally found a black undertaker who cremated him for a thousand dollars, no questions asked.

(NED *crosses to* BRUCE *and embraces him;* BRUCE *puts his arms around* NED.)

BRUCE:   Would you and Felix mind if I spent the night on your sofa? Just one night. I don't want to go home.

# Scene 12

EMMA *sits alone in a spotlight, facing a doctor who stands at a distance, perhaps in the audience. She holds a number of files on her lap, or they are placed in a carrier attached to her wheelchair.*

EXAMINING DOCTOR: Dr. Brookner, the government's position is this. There are several million dollars in the pipeline, five to be exact, for which we have received some fifty-five million dollars' worth of requests—all the way from a doctor in North Dakota who desires to study the semen of pigs to the health reporter on Long Island who is convinced this is being transmitted by dogs and the reason so many gay men are contracting it is because they have so many dogs.

EMMA: Five million dollars doesn't seem quite right for some two thousand cases. The government spent twenty million investigating seven deaths from Tylenol. We are now almost into the third year of this epidemic.

EXAMINING DOCTOR: Unfortunately the President has threatened to veto. As you know, he's gone on record as being unalterably and irrevocably opposed to anything that might be construed as an endorsement of homosexuality. Naturally, this has slowed things down.

EMMA: Naturally. It looks like we've got a pretty successful stalemate going on here.

EXAMINING DOCTOR: Well, that's not what we're here to discuss today, is it?

EMMA:   I don't think I'm going to enjoy hearing what I think I'm about to hear. But go ahead. At your own peril.

EXAMINING DOCTOR:   We have decided to reject your application for funding.

EMMA:   Oh? I would like to hear your reasons.

EXAMINING DOCTOR:   We felt the direction of your thinking was imprecise and unfocused.

EMMA:   Could you be a little more precise?

EXAMINING DOCTOR:   I beg your pardon?

EMMA:   You don't know what's going on any more than I do. My guess is as good as anybody's. Why are you blocking my efforts?

EXAMINING DOCTOR:   Dr. Brookner, since you first became involved with this—and we pay tribute to you as a pioneer, one of the few courageous pioneers—there have been other investigators . . . Quite frankly, it's no longer just your disease, though you seem to think it is.

EMMA:   Oh, I do, do I? And you're here to take it away from me, is that it? Well, I'll let you in on a little secret, doctor. You can have it. I didn't want it in the first place. You think it's my good fortune to have the privilege of watching young men die? Oh, what's the use! What am I arguing with you for? You don't know enough medicine to treat a mouse. You don't know enough science to study boiled water. How dare you come and judge me?

EXAMINING DOCTOR:   We only serve on this panel at the behest of Dr. Joost.

EMMA:   Another idiot. And, by the way, a closeted homosexual who is doing everything in his power to sweep this under the rug, and I vowed I'd never say that in public. How does it always happen that all the idiots are always on your team? You guys have all the money, call the shots, shut everybody out, and then operate behind closed doors. I am taking care of more victims of this epidemic than anyone in the world. We have more accumulated test results, more data, more frozen blood samples, more experience! How can you not fund my research or invite me to participate in yours? A promising virus has already been discovered—in France. Why are we being told not to cooperate with the French? Why are you refusing to cooperate with the French? Just so you can steal a Nobel Prize? Your National Institutes of Health received my first request for research money two years ago. It took you one year just to print up application forms. It's taken you two and a half years from my first reported case just to show up here to take a look. The paltry amount of money you are making us beg for—from the four billion dollars you are given each and every year—won't come to anyone until only God knows when. Any way you add all this up, it is an unconscionable delay and has never, never existed in any other health emergency during this entire century. While something is being passed around that causes death. We are enduring an epidemic of death. Women have been discovered to have it in Africa—where it is clearly transmitted heterosexually. It is only a question of time. We could all be dead before you do anything. You want my patients? Take them! TAKE THEM! (*She starts hurling her folders and papers at him, out into space.*) Just do something for them! You're fucking right I'm imprecise and unfocused. And you are all idiots!

# Scene 13

*A big empty room, which will be the organization's new offices.* BRUCE *is walking around by himself.* NED *comes in from upstairs.*

NED:   This is perfect for our new offices. The room upstairs is just as big. And it's cheap.

BRUCE:   How come, do you think?

NED:   Didn't Tommy tell you? After he found it, he ran into the owner in a gay bar who confessed, after a few beers, his best friend is sick. Did you see us on TV picketing the Mayor yesterday in all that rain?

BRUCE:   Yes.

NED:   How'd we look?

BRUCE:   All wet.

NED:   He's got four more hours to go. Our letter threatened if he didn't meet with us by the end of the day we'd escalate the civil disobedience. Mel found this huge straight black guy who trained with Martin Luther King. He's teaching us how to tie up the bridge and tunnel traffic. Don't worry— a bunch of us are doing this on our own.

BRUCE:   Tommy got the call.

NED:   Tommy? Why didn't you tell me? When did they call?

BRUCE:   This morning.

NED:   When's the meeting?

BRUCE:   Tomorrow.

NED:   You see. It works! What time?

BRUCE: Eight A.M.

NED: For the Mayor I'll get up early.

BRUCE: We can only bring ten people. Hiram's orders.

NED: Who's going?

BRUCE: The Community Council sends two, the Network sends two, the Task Force sends two, we send two, and two patients.

NED: I'll pick you up at seven-thirty and we can share a cab.

BRUCE: You remember we elected Tommy executive director.

NED: I'm going.

BRUCE: We can only bring two.

NED: You just call Hiram and tell him we're bringing three.

BRUCE: The list of names has already been phoned in. It's too late.

NED: So I'll just go. What are they going to do? Kick me out? Already phoned in? Too late? Why is everything so final? Why is all this being done behind my back? How dare you make this decision without consulting me?

BRUCE: Ned...

NED: I wrote that letter, I got sixty gay organizations to sign it, I organized the picketing when the Mayor wouldn't respond, that meeting is mine! It's happening because of me! It took me twenty-one months to arrange it and, God damn it, I'm going to go!

BRUCE: You're not the whole organization.

NED: What does that mean? Why didn't Tommy tell me?

BRUCE: I told him not to.

NED:   You what?

BRUCE:   I wanted to poll the board.

NED:   Behind my back—what kind of betrayal is going on behind my back? I'm on the board, you didn't poll me. I am going to that meeting representing this organization that I have spent every minute of my life fighting for and that was started in my living room, or I quit!

BRUCE:   I told them I didn't think you'd accept their decision.

NED:   (*As it sinks in.*) You would let me quit? You didn't have to poll the board. If you wanted to take me, you'd take me. I embarrass you.

BRUCE:   Yes, you do. The Mayor's finally meeting with us and we all feel we now have a chance to—

NED:   A chance to kiss his ass?

BRUCE:   We want to work from the inside now that we have the contact.

NED:   It won't work. Did you get this meeting by kissing his ass? He's the one person most responsible for letting this epidemic get so out of control. If he'd responded with one ounce of compassion when we first tried to reach him, we'd have saved two years. You'll see... We have over half a million dollars. The *Times* is finally writing about us. Why are you willing to let me go when I've been so effective? When you need me most?

BRUCE:   You... you're a bully. If the board doesn't agree with you, you always threaten to leave. You never listen to us. I can't work with you anymore.

NED:   And you're strangling this organization with your fear and your conservatism. The organization I promised everyone would fight for them isn't fighting at all. It's become the gay est.

BRUCE: Maybe that's what it wanted to become. Maybe that's all it could become. You can't turn something into something it doesn't want to become. We just feel you can't tell people how to live.

NED: Drop that! Just drop it! The cases are still doubling every six months. Of course we have to tell people how to live. Or else there won't be any people left! Did you ever consider it could get so bad they'll quarantine us or put us in camps?

BRUCE: Oh, they will not.

NED: It's happened before. It's all happened before. History is worth shit. I swear to God I now understand . . . Is this how so many people just walked into gas chambers? But at least they identified themselves to each other and to the world.

BRUCE: You can't call people gay who don't want to be.

NED: Bruce—after you're dead, it doesn't make any difference.

BRUCE: (*Takes a letter out of his pocket.*) The board wanted me to read you this letter. "We are circulating this letter widely among people of judgment and good sense in our community. We take this action to try to combat your damage, wrought, so far as we can see, by your having no scruples whatever. You are on a colossal ego trip we must curtail. To manipulate fear, as you have done repeatedly in your 'merchandising' of this epidemic, is to us the gesture of barbarism. To exploit the deaths of gay men, as you have done in publications all over America, is to us an act of inexcusable vandalism. And to attempt to justify your bursts of outrageous temper as 'part of what it means to be Jewish' is past our comprehending. And, after years of liberation, you have helped make sex dirty again for us—terrible and forbidden. We are more angry at you than ever in our lives toward anyone. We think you want to lead us all. Well, we do not want you to. In accordance with our by-laws as drawn up by Weeks, Frankel, Levinstein, Mr. Ned Weeks is hereby removed as a director. We beg that you leave us quietly and not destroy us and what good work we manage despite your disapproval. In closing, please know we always welcome your input, advice, and help."

(BRUCE *tries to hand* NED *the letter.* NED *won't take it.* BRUCE *tries to put it in* NED's *breast pocket.* NED *deflects* BRUCE's *hand.*)

NED:    I belong to a culture that includes Proust, Henry James, Tchaikovsky, Cole Porter, Plato, Socrates, Aristotle, Alexander the Great, Michaelangelo, Leonardo da Vinci, Christopher Marlowe, Walt Whitman, Herman Melville, Tennessee Williams, Byron, E.M. Forster, Lorca, Auden, Francis Bacon, James Baldwin, Harry Stack Sullivan, John Maynard Keynes, Dag Hammarskjold . . . These are not invisible men. Poor Bruce. Poor frightened Bruce. Once upon a time you wanted to be a soldier. Bruce, did you know that it was an openly gay Englishman who was as responsible as any man for winning the Second World War? His name was Alan Turing and he cracked the Germans' Enigma code so the Allies knew in advance what the Nazis were going to do—and when the war was over he committed suicide he was so hounded for being gay. Why don't they teach any of this in the schools? If they did, maybe he wouldn't have killed himself and maybe you wouldn't be so terrified of who you are. The only way we'll have real pride is when we demand recognition of a culture that isn't just sexual. It's all there—all through history we've been there; but we have to claim it, and identify who was in it, and articulate what's in our minds and hearts and all our creative contributions to this earth. And until we do that, and until we organize ourselves block by neighborhood by city by state into a united visible community that fights back, we're doomed. That's how I want to be defined: as one of the men who fought the war. Being defined by our cocks is literally killing us. Must we all be reduced to becoming our own murderers? Why couldn't you and I, Bruce Niles and Ned Weeks, have been leaders in creating a new definition of what it means to be gay? I blame myself as much as you. Bruce, I know I'm an asshole. But, please, I beg you, don't shut me out.

(BRUCE *starts to leave then stops and comes to Ned. He puts his hand on his cheek, perhaps kisses him, and then leaves him standing alone.*)

# Scene 14

NED's *apartment.* FELIX *is sitting on the floor. He has been eating junk food.* NED *comes in carrying a bag of groceries.*

NED:  Why are you sitting on the floor?

FELIX:  I fell down trying to get from there to here.

NED:  Let's put you to bed.

FELIX:  Don't touch me! I'm so ugly. I cannot stand it when you look at my body.

NED:  Did you go to chemo today?

FELIX:  Yes. I threw it all up. You don't have to let me stay here with you. This is horrible for you.

NED:    (*Touching* FELIX's *hair.*) No fallout yet. Phil looks cute shaved. I'm hungry. How about you? Can you eat a little? Please. You've got to eat. Soup... something light... I've bought dinner.

FELIX:    Emma says a cure won't come until the next century. Emma says it's years till a vaccine, which won't do me any good anyway. Emma says the incubation period might be up to three, ten, twenty years.

NED:    Emma says you've got to eat.

FELIX:    I looked at all my datebooks and no one else I slept with is sick. That I know of. Maybe it was you. Maybe you've been a carrier for twenty years. Or maybe now you only have three years to go.

NED:    Felix, we don't need to do this again to each other.

FELIX:    Whoever thought you'd die from having sex?

NED:    Did Emma also tell you that research at the NIH has finally started. That something is now possible. We have to hope.

FELIX:    Oh, do we?

NED:    Yes, we do.

FELIX:    And how am I supposed to do that? You Jewish boys who think you can always make everything right—that the world can always be a better place. Did I tell you the *Times* is running an editorial this Sunday entitled "The Slow Response"? And you're right: I didn't have anything to do with it.

NED:    Why are you doing this? Why are you eating this shit? Twinkies, potato chips... You know how important it is to watch your nutrition. You're supposed to eat right.

FELIX:    I have a life expectancy of ten more minutes I'm going to eat what I want to eat. Ned, it's going to get messier any day now and I don't want to make you see it.

NED: Nobody makes me do anything; you should know that better than anybody else by now. What are you going to do? Sit on the floor for the rest of your life? We have a bed in the other room. You could listen to those relaxation tapes we bought you three months ago. You haven't used them at all. Do you hear me?

FELIX: Yes, I hear you. That guy David who sold you the pig on Bleecker Street finally died. He took forever. They say he looked like someone out of Auschwitz. Do you hear me?

NED: No. Are you ready to get up yet? And eat something?

FELIX: No!—I've had over forty treatments. No!—I've had three, no four different types of chemo. No!—I've had interferon, a couple kinds. I've had two different experimentals. Emma has spent more time on me than anyone else. None of it has done a thing. I've had to go into the hospital four times—and please God don't make me go back into the hospital until I die. My illness has cost my—no! the *New Yorks Times'* insurance company over $300,000. Eighty-five percent of us are dead after two years, Alexander; it gets higher after three. Emma has lost so many patients they call her Dr. Death. You cannot force the goddamn sun to come out.

NED: Felix, I am so sick of statistics, and numbers, and body counts, and how-manys, and Emma; and everyday, Felix, there are only more numbers, and fights—I am so sick of fighting, and bragging about fighting, and everybody's stupidity, and blindness, and intransigence, and guilt trips. You can't eat the food? Don't eat the food. Take your poison. I don't care. You can't get up off the floor—fine, stay there. I don't care. Fish—fish is good for you; we don't want any of that, do we? (*Item by item, he throws the food on the floor.*) No green salad. No broccoli; we don't want any of that, no, sir. No bread with seven grains. Who would ever want any milk? You might get some calcium in your bones. (*The carton of milk explodes when it hits the floor.*) You want to die, Felix? Die!

(NED *retreats to a far corner. After a moment,* FELIX *crawls through the milk, takes an item of food, which he pulls along with his hand, and with extreme effort makes his way across to* NED. *They fall into each other's arms.*)

NED:   Felix, please don't leave me.

## Scene 15

BEN'*s office.* FELIX, *with great effort, walks toward him. Though he looks terrible,* FELIX *has a bit of his old twinkle.*

FELIX:   Thank you for seeing me. Your brother and I are lovers. I'm dying and I need to make a will. Oh, I know Neddie hasn't been talking to you; our excuse is we've sort of been preoccupied. It's a little hard on us, isn't it, his kind of love, because we disappoint him so. But it is love. I hope you know that. I haven't very much time left. I want to leave everything to Ned. I've written it all down.

BEN:   (*Taking the piece of paper from* FELIX *and studying it.*) Do you have any family, Felix?

FELIX:   My parents are dead. I had a wife.

BEN: You had a wife?

FELIX: Yes. Here's the divorce. (*He hands* BEN *another piece of paper.*) And I have a son. Here's . . . she has custody. (*He hands over yet another piece of paper.*)

BEN: Does she know you're ill?

FELIX: Yes. I called and we've said our good-byes. She doesn't want anything from me. She was actually rather pleasant. Although she wouldn't let me talk to my boy.

BEN: How is my brother?

FELIX: Well, he blames himself, of course, for everything from my dying to the state of the entire world. But he's not talking so much these days, believe it or not. You must be as stubborn as he is—not to have called.

BEN: I think of doing it every day. I'm sorry I didn't know you were ill. I'll call him right away.

FELIX: He's up at Yale for the week. He's in terrible shape. He was thrown out of the organization he loved so much. After almost three years he sits at home all day, flagellating himself awfully because he thinks he's failed some essential test—plus my getting near the end and you two still not talking to each other.

BEN: Ned was thrown out of his own organization?

FELIX: Yes.

BEN: Felix, I wish we could have met sooner.

FELIX: I haven't much, except a beautiful piece of land on the Cape in Wellfleet on a hill overlooking the Atlantic Ocean. Ned doesn't know about it. It was to have been a surprise, we'd live there together in the house he always wanted. I also have an insurance policy with the *Times*. I'm a reporter for the *New York Times*.

BEN:  You work for the *Times*?

FELIX:  Yes. Fashion. La-de-da. It's meant to come to my next of kin. I've specified Ned. I'm afraid they might not give it to him.

BEN:  If he is listed as the beneficiary, they must.

FELIX:  But what if they don't?

BEN:  I assure you I will fight to see that he gets it.

FELIX:  I was hoping you'd say that. Can I sign my will now, please, in case I don't have time to see you again?

BEN:  This will be quite legal. We can stop by one of my associates' offices and get it properly witnessed as you sign it.

FELIX:  My little piece of paper is legal? Then why did you go to law school?

BEN:  I sometimes wonder. You know, Felix, I think of leaving here, too, because I don't think anybody is listening to me either. And I set all this up as well. (*A hospital bed is wheeled into stage center by two orderlies, wearing masks and gloves.*) I understand that the virus has finally been discovered in Washington.

FELIX:  The story is they couldn't find it, so after fifteen months they stole it from the French and renamed it. With who knows how many million of us now exposed... Oh, there is not a good word to be said for anybody's behavior in this whole mess. Then could you help me get a taxi, please? I have to get to the airport.

BEN:  The airport?

FELIX:  I'm going to Rumania to see their famous woman doctor. A desperation tactic, Tommy would call it. Does flying Bucharest Airlines inspire you with any confidence?

# Scene 16

FELIX's *hospital room*. FELIX *lies in bed*. NED *enters*.

FELIX:   I should be wearing something white.

NED:   You are.

FELIX:   It should be something Perry Ellis ran up for me personally.

NED:   (*As* FELIX *presses a piece of rock into his hand*.) What's this?

FELIX:   From my trip. I forgot to give it to you. This is a piece of rock from Dracula's castle.

NED:   Reminded you of me, did it?

FELIX:   To remind you of me. Please learn to fight again.

NED:   I went to a meeting at the Bishop's. All the gay leaders were there, including Bruce and Tommy. I wasn't allowed in. I went in to the men's room of the rectory and the Bishop came in and as we stood there peeing side by side I screamed at him, "What kind of house of God are we in?"

FELIX:   Don't lose that anger. Just have a little more patience and forgiveness. For yourself as well.

NED:   What am I ever going to do without you?

FELIX:   Finish writing something. Okay?

NED:   Okay.

FELIX:   Promise?

NED:   I promise.

FELIX:   Okay. It better be good.

(BEN *enters the scene.*)

FELIX:   Hello, Ben.

BEN:   Hello, Felix.

(*Before* NED *can do more than register his surprise at seeing* BEN, EMMA *enters and comes to the side of the bed.*)

FELIX:   Emma, could we start, please.

EMMA:   We are gathered here in the sight of God to join together these two men. They love each other very much and want to be married in the presence of their family before Felix dies. I can see no objection. This is my hospital, my church. Do you, Felix Turner, take Ned Weeks—

FELIX:   Alexander.

EMMA:   . . . to be your . . .

FELIX:   My lover. My lover. I do.

NED:   I do.

(FELIX *is dead.* EMMA, *who has been holding Felix's hand and monitoring his pulse, places his hand on his body. She leaves. The two orderlies enter and push the hospital bed, through all the accumulated mess, off stage.*)

NED:   He always wanted me to take him to your new house in the country. Just the four of us.

BEN:   Ned, I'm sorry. For Felix . . . and for other things.

NED:   Why didn't I fight harder! Why didn't I picket the White House, all by myself if nobody would come. Or go on a hunger strike. I forgot to tell him something. Felix, when they invited me to Gay Week at Yale, they had a dance . . . In my old college dining hall, just across the campus from that tiny freshman room where I wanted to kill myself because I thought I was the only gay man in the world—they had a dance. Felix, there were six hundred young men and women there. Smart, exceptional young men and women. Thank you, Felix.

(*After a moment,* BEN *crosses to* NED, *and somehow they manage to kiss and embrace and hold on to each other.*)


# THE END

PLUME

# COMING OF AGE

PLUME

# NOVELS OF GENIUS AND PASSION

# NEW VOICES

☐ **WALTZ IN MARATHON by Charles Dickinson.** Harry Waltz, a widower with grown children, is the richest man in Marathon, Michigan. He lives alone and likes it—until his orderly life begins to shift and alter. Most astonishing of all, Waltz falls in love with an attractive attorney—with consequences that astonish them both.     (255937—$6.95)

☐ **FAMOUS ALL OVER TOWN by Danny Santiago.** This is the Los Angeles of the Chicano barrio, where everything is stacked against the teen-aged hero, Chato Medina, his beleaguered family, his defiant and doomed friends, and the future he may not make it far enough to enjoy. Chato, however, is out to beat all the odds—his own way . . .
(255112—$6.95)

☐ **BACK EAST by Ellen Pall.** Melanie Armour is leaving L.A. to go to New York. There she meets Lucian Curry, a young actor, and at the height of their involvement, Melanie goes to her brother-in-law's wedding in Maine—where a family crisis forces her to make a bittersweet decision.     (255910—$7.95)

☐ **FLIGHTS by Jim Shepard.** Biddy Siebert is failing math and life. Lost in an endless series of dice baseball games. Biddy even daydreams about strikeouts and fumbles—until he sees a chance to do something right . . . and concocts a brilliantly loopy flight plan for growing up in a hurry.     (255929—$6.95)

Prices slightly higher in Canada.
To order use coupon on next page.

PLUME

# THE FINEST IN SHORT FICTION